THE ARTIFICIAL SILK GIRL
Irmgard Keun

translated by Kathie von Ankum
introduction by Maria Tatar

OTHER

Other Press • New York

Original title: *Das kunstseidene Mädchen*, © Econ Ullstein List
Verlag GmbH & Co. KG, Munich. Published 1992 by Claassen
Verlag.

Translation copyright © 2002 Kathie von Ankum

Production Editor: Robert D. Hack

Book design: Terry Berkowitz with Kaoru Tamura

This book was set in 11 pt. Electra LH Regular by Alpha Graphics
of Pittsfield, NH.

10 9 8 7 6 5 4 3 2

Library of Congress Cataloging-in-Publication Data

Keun, Irmgard, 1910–
    [Kunstseidene Mädchen. English]
    The artificial silk girl / by Irmgard Keun ; translated into
English by Kathie von Ankum.
        p. cm.
    ISBN 1-892746-81-6; 1-59051-078-X (pbk.)
    I. Title.
PT2621.E92 K813 2002
833'.912—dc21   2001058023

CONTENTS

PUBLISHER'S NOTE

Other Press wants to thank Kathie von Ankum for her elegant translation and for her unflagging commitment to *The Artificial Silk Girl*, without which this crucial work would not have been reintroduced to the English-speaking world.

TRANSLATOR'S NOTE

When *The Artificial Silk Girl* first appeared in English in 1933, it was part of an ongoing cultural exchange between Germany and Great Britain. But it was not only the fact that Keun's novel had been a bestseller in Germany that prompted its instant translation; it was also one of the last accounts of everyday German life before the Nazis came to power. By the time the English translation appeared in Great Britain, Keun's books had already been banned in Germany. Thus star translator Basil Creighton made a special point of emphasizing the political environment encountered by Keun's *Artificial Silk Girl* in Berlin, adding passages in the translation that were designed specifically to help readers position Keun's novel in the context of then-recent German political developments.

While there can be no doubt about Keun's anti-Nazi sentiment, her "artificial silk girl" doesn't really have any political convictions. In fact, she is completely clueless when it comes to politics, and therefore a perfect example for so many Germans of that time who realized what they had gotten caught up in only when it was too late to do much about it. In that sense, *The Artificial Silk Girl* can be read as an historical document, an entertaining and disturbing account of what it was like to be a young woman in Berlin as the Golden Twenties were drawing to a close.

But to my mind, such an historical reading is only of secondary importance for the modern reader. What makes us identify with Keun's protagonist Doris is not so much the fact that she is a classic example of the German "bystander," but rather that she is the quintessential "material girl." Doris may not understand the headlines of the daily papers, but she does understand the message of the illustrated press mandating her to mold her life after the glamorous models presented on the movie screen and on the pages of glossy magazines she reads every day. In her desperate pursuit of this kind of happiness, her effort to become the flesh and blood rendition of those media icons, Doris features as a predecessor of the Bridget Joneses, the Carrie Bradshaws, and the shopaholic Rebecca Bloomwoods of our day.

The historical and cultural parameters may have changed. However, the basic message remains the same: women have entered the professional world. They are expected to stand on their own feet. But their standard of living continues to depend on a husband's income, and hence they and the world around them continue to measure their success by their ability to get a man to commit. This requires a serious investment in personal appearance, the ability to "play stupid" when necessary, and a willingness to deny their own emotional needs—all in an effort to acquire a relationship that will assure the life that is held out by the media as the only one worth living.

The critical response to this message made Keun a bestselling author in the 1930s—just as Helen Fielding, Candace Bushnell, and Sophie Kinsella are today. It is mainly for this reason that I think it is important to make a fresh English translation of Keun's *The Artificial Silk Girl* accessible to audiences now.

Kathie von Ankum
New York City, 2001

INTRODUCTION

Doris, the artificial silk girl in the title of Irmgard Keun's acclaimed novel, is a collector of images: "I walk around the streets and the restaurants and among people and lanterns. And then I try to remember what I've seen." If the narrator of Christopher Isherwood's "Goodbye to Berlin" achieved acclaim by declaring, "I am a camera," Doris, too, insists that she works in a visual rather than verbal medium. She may "write everything down," but she feels nothing but contempt for diarists, who traffic in mere words. "I want to write like a movie," she declares, offering continuous reels rather than mere snapshots of the world she inhabits. If Doris is unable to script her life in exactly the way she desires, she nonetheless succeeds in producing powerful images that enlarge our understanding of the culture of everyday life in an era that came to be known as the "golden twenties."

With her focus on surfaces, appearances, skins, faces, and façades, Doris self-consciously sets herself against the literary tradition of confessional narratives. She has no intention of baring her soul, interrogating her motives, or expressing her feelings. One of her first descriptive moves is trained on her body rather than on what goes on in her mind: "I'm sitting in my room in my nightgown, which has slipped off my famous shoulder, and everything about me is just first class — only my left leg is slightly wider than my right one." It is no accident that Doris's story begins with the theft of a fur coat. ("I felt like kissing it, that's how much I loved it.") That transgression changes her life, marking a transition from home (a place that offers intimacy, even if in somewhat troubled form) to the big city (an arena in which she will judge and be judged by surface appearances alone). With her second skin, Doris leaves behind what is presumably the town of Cologne to seek her fortune in the city of Berlin.

In Cologne, Doris had worked as an actress on a small stage, reciting a single line from a play by the renowned German dramatist Friedrich Schiller. In Berlin, she attempts to move beyond bit parts and to fashion herself into a screen idol, hoping to enter Berlin's cinematic culture but also seeking to become an icon of seductive glamour in her own film. Doris is unable to realize the Hollywood dream, to star in the master narrative that will take her from rags to riches. The constant friction between her materialistic desires and her romantic ambitions derails efforts to become upward mobile. It is as if Doris has joined the cast of a play by the Viennese dramatist Arthur Schnitzler. At once naive and cynical, innocent and corrupt, she experiences life as a series of "episodes," short-term affairs — bitter and sweet, in varying proportions — that lead nowhere.

If Doris fails to plot her life along the lines of Hollywood melodrama, she nonetheless succeeds in producing a document in the cinematic style (*Kinostil*) endorsed by the celebrated novelist Alfred Döblin, the Berlin physician who was also one of Weimar Germany's leading intellectuals. Doris becomes a camera, recording the sights and sounds of city life. Her affair with Brenner, a blind veteran, becomes an opportunity for intensifying her power of vision. To Brenner's question "What did you see?" Doris responds with the visual acuity of the artist George Grosz. "I saw — men standing at corners selling perfume, without a coat and a pert face and a gray cap on — and posters with naked and rosy girls on them and nobody looking at them . . . . I saw — a man with a sign around his neck, 'I will accept any work' with 'any' underlined three times in red — and a spiteful mouth, the corners of which were drawn increasingly down."

When Doris takes Brenner out for a night on the town, she evokes Berlin nightlife with its heady distractions and cheerless glamour. Wandering through the streets, stopping at cafes and restaurants, Doris desperately seeks to persuade herself and Brenner that Berlin has the power to energize and invigorate with its myriad diversions. "I just want him to like my Berlin." But Doris's power of vision, despite its relentless focus on surfaces, ends by penetrating through to what lies beneath the surface entertainments. "The city isn't good and the city isn't happy and the city is sick," Brenner concludes after seeing Berlin through Doris's eyes. Like George Grosz's sketches of street scenes and night life, Doris's account exposes existential anxiety and icy estrangement. "And sometimes somebody is laughing — and that laugh is stuffing all of yesterday's and today's anger back into the mouth that it's oozing from." Uncovering the pathologies of urban life through her laser-like vision, she herself ends by feeling physically and spiritually depleted.

Doris's departure from home begins as a kind of fairy-tale adventure. Like the heroine of the Grimms' fairy tale "Allerleirauh," she leaves home wearing a pelt as disguise and makes her way through the world looking for a second home. But the artificial silk girl fails to emerge as a triumphant fairy-tale heroine and becomes a double of Hans Christian Andersen's little match girl, homeless and exposed to the elements in a physically and spiritually chilling site on Christmas night. "I'm freezing to death with loneliness," she declares, shortly before spending the night on a park bench. In a rare confessional moment, Doris avows that her goal is to find a way home: "Every human being is like a stove for my heart that is homesick but not always longing for my parents' house, but for a real home." The fairy-tale dream of establishing a new home is shattered by the grim realities of urban life.

That Doris discovers real companionship in her relationship to a war veteran is no coincidence. The veteran and the prostitute, both figures of ill repute, operated powerfully in Weimar Germany's cultural imaginary. Positioned on the periphery of society, they served a central symbolic role in representations of modern life. Doris may not descend into hard-core prostitution, but she turns briefly to streetwalking and aligns herself with the abject culture of begging for a living. If she feels superior to the beggars on the street, it is only because she uses her body to attract attention and desire rather than empathy and revulsion. Yet she is also supremely aware that only a few years separate the beggars from the prostitutes. Walking the streets during a time of prosperity, she sees "lots of men around selling matches and shoelaces — so many of them — and everywhere there are whores in the streets, and young men with starved voices," and she makes sure to give "everyone" a token handout.

Keun's compelling rendering of Berlin in the 1920s was inspired in part by Alfred Döblin's *Berlin Alexanderplatz* (1929), a work that had created a literary sensation by turning the spotlight on convicts, prostitutes, and criminal lowlifes. Döblin met Keun at a reading in Cologne and encouraged her to write, emphasizing that her sharp powers of observation and narrative skills could lead to real literary prominence. Following Döblin's example, along with that of Brecht, who had portrayed armies of beggars, prostitutes, and gangsters in his popular *Threepenny Opera* (1928), Keun turned her attention to giving a voice to those who had never had any real literary representation. While male authors had sought to ventriloquize female characters — Arthur Schnitzler's *Fräulein Else* is perhaps the most notorious example — few women had engaged their literary skills to solving the problem of female representation in contemporary literature. Inspired by the example of Anita Loos's *Gentlemen Prefer Blondes* (1925), Keun set out to write the German answer to the bestselling novel from the United States.

In giving us the dark underside of the glamorous "golden twenties," Keun came to be decried as an exponent of what the Nazis called "asphalt literature with anti-German tendencies." But what disturbed the Nazis about Keun's *Artificial Silk Girl* was not merely its evocation of urban pathologies, but also its endorsement of empathy and tolerance. Looking for distraction, Doris goes to the movies with Ernest (the "Green Moss") and sees *Girls in Uniform*, a film that had its world premier in Berlin in 1931. Directed by the actress Leontine Sagan, the film chronicles the events leading to the near suicide of a young woman at a German boarding school. Manuela, a newly arrived student, develops emotional and erotic feelings for one of her teachers, and is driven to the brink of suicide by the headmistress, a woman associated with militarism. The film ends on a conciliatory note, with a headmistress so shaken by the events that she is prepared to make real reforms.

Doris reacts with sympathy to Manuela's plight, just as she empathizes with those who share her fate on the streets. "You love somebody and that brings tears to your eyes and gives you a red nose. It doesn't matter whether it's a man or a woman of God." In this empathetic identification with a lesbian protagonist, Doris reveals herself to be, if not a shrewd social critic, then at least an exponent of open-mindedness and tolerance. It was this message about our common humanity more than the novel's gritty realism that must have given offense to Nazi censorship boards.

In 1933, Irmgard Keun's writings were banned. *The Artificial Silk Girl* was withdrawn from publication, with all remaining copies destroyed. Disturbed by the ease with which both her husband and her brother made the transition to a new political regime, Keun found herself anxious and distraught, unable to continue writing. "Do I know where I'll be tomorrow? If it were just a matter of talent, accomplishment, hard work, then I wouldn't be afraid. The idea of risk doesn't bother me. I know what risk is. But how do I deal with senseless arbitrary decisions?" she wrote in a letter of 1933. In 1936, she left her husband, who encouraged her to flee with "the Negroes and the Jews" and traveled to Belgium, where she could "write, speak, and breathe once again." In Ostende she joined a circle of exiles that included Joseph Roth, with whom she had a two-yearlong affair.

After two months in New York, Keun returned to Germany illegally under the name Charlotte Tralow. Although she resumed writing, she remained socially isolated, even after the birth of her daughter in 1951. Although she was rediscovered as a writer in the mid-1970s, she remained indifferent to media attention. She died at home in Cologne in 1982.

Further Reading on Irmgard Keun's *The Artificial Silk Girl*

For a fuller analysis of Keun's novel, readers will want to consult the essays listed below.

Katharina von Ankum (1994). "Material Girls: Consumer Culture and the 'New Woman' in Anita Loos' *Gentlemen Prefer Blondes* and Irmgard Keun's *Das kunstseidene Mädchen." Colloquia Germanica* 27:159–172.

Katharina von Ankum (1997). "Gendered Urban Spaces in Irmgard Keun's *Das kunstseidene Mädchen.*" In *Women and the Metropolis: Gender and Modernity in Weimar Culture.* Berkeley, CA: University of California Press, pp. 162–184.

Leo A. Lensing (1985). "Cinema, Society, and Literature in Irmgard Keun's *Das kunstseidene Mädchen.*" *Germanic Review* 60:129–134.

1

THE END OF SUMMER AND THE MID-SIZE TOWN

It must have been around twelve midnight last night that I felt something wonderful happening inside of me. I was in bed — I had meant to wash my feet, but I was too tired after that hectic night the day before, and hadn't I told Therese: "You don't get anything out of letting yourself be talked to on the street. You owe yourself some self-respect, after all."

Besides, I already knew the program at the *Kaiserhof*. And then all this drinking — I had trouble getting home all right, and it's never easy for me to say no in the first place. "The day after tomorrow, then," I told him. But no way! A guy with knobby fingers like that and always just ordering the cheap wine from the top of the menu, and cigarettes at five pfennigs apiece — when a man starts out that way, where is it going to end?

And then I felt so sick at the office, and the old man isn't rolling in dough anymore either, and could fire me any day. So tonight I went straight home and to bed, without washing my feet. Didn't wash my neck either. And as I was lying there and my whole body was asleep already, only my eyes were still open — and the white moonlight was shining on my head, and I was thinking how nice that goes with my black hair and what a shame Hubert can't see me like that, when he's the only one, after all, whom I've ever loved. And then I felt the aura of Hubert surrounding me, and the moon was shining and I could hear a gramophone playing next door, and then something wonderful happened inside of me — as had happened before, but never anything like this. I felt like writing a poem, but that might have had to rhyme and I was too tired for that. But I realized that there is something unusual about me. Hubert had felt it too, and Fräulein Vogelsang from my school as well, after I presented them with a rendition of *Erlkönig* that knocked their socks off. And I'm quite different from Therese and all those other girls at the office and the rest of them, who never have anything wonderful going on inside them. Plus I speak almost without dialect, which makes a difference, and gives me a special touch, particularly since my father and mother speak with a dialect that I find nothing short of embarrassing.

And I think it will be a good thing if I write everything down, because I'm an unusual person. I don't mean a diary — that's ridiculous for a trendy girl like me. But I want to write like a movie, because my life is like that and it's going to become even more so. And I look like Colleen Moore, if she had a perm and her nose were a little more fashionable, like pointing up. And when I read it later on, everything will be like at the movies — I'm looking at myself in pictures. And now I'm sitting in my room in my nightgown, which has slipped off my famous shoulder, and everything about me is just first class — only my left leg is slightly wider than my right one. But only slightly. It's very cold, but it's nicer being in your nightgown — otherwise I'd put on my coat.

And it will do me good to be writing without commas for a change, and real language — not that unnatural stuff from the office. And for every comma that's missing, I have to give that old beanstalk of an attorney — he has pimples too, and his skin looks like my old yellow leather purse without a zipper, I'm ashamed to have it on me when I'm in decent company — that's the kind of skin he has. Anyway, I don't think much of attorneys — always money-grubbing and talking big with nothing behind it. I pretend not to notice, since my father is out of work and my mother works at the theater, which you also can't count on these days. But I was talking about the beanstalk. So I put the letters in front of him, and for every missing comma, I give him this sensual look. And I can smell trouble already, because I'm getting tired of it. But I'm sure I can keep him off my back for another four weeks; I always tell him that my father is so strict, and I have to go home right away. But when a man gets wild, there's no more excuses — I know what I'm talking about. And he's bound to get worked up in time, considering my sensual looks at every missing comma. True education has nothing to do with commas! Not that there's anything going on between him and me. As I've been telling Therese, who also works at the office and is my friend: "There has to be some love involved. Otherwise, what about our ideals?"

And Therese told me that she too has ideals, because she's faithful to a married man who doesn't have a penny and is not even thinking of divorce and has moved to Goslar — and she's all dried up and turned 38 last weekend — although she only admits to 30, but looks like 40 — and all because of that Mr. Boring. Well, I'm not that much into ideals. I can't see the point of it.

And I bought myself a thick black notebook and cut some doves out of white paper and stuck them on the cover, and now I'm looking for a beginning. My name is Doris, and I'm baptized and Christian, and born too. We are living in the year 1931. Tomorrow, I'll write more.

I had a good day, because it was my last one and getting paid just does one good, even though I have to give

70 of my 120 — Therese gets 20 more — to my father, who just gets drunk on it, because he's unemployed right now and has nothing else to do. But I immediately bought a hat for myself with the 50 marks I had left, with a feather and in forest green — that's this season's fashion color, and it goes fabulously well with my rosy complexion. And wearing it off to the side is just so chic, and I already had a forest green coat made for myself — tailored with a fox collar — a present from Käsemann, who absolutely almost wanted to marry me. But I didn't. Because in the long run, I'm too good for the short and stocky type, particularly if they're called Käsemann. But now my outfit is complete, which is the most important thing for a girl who wants to get ahead and has ambition.

And I'm sitting in a café right now — a cup of coffee is something I can afford on my own today. I like the music they're playing: *The Gypsy Baron* or *Aida* — it doesn't really matter. There's a man with a girl sitting next to me. He's something more elegant — but not too — and she has a face like a turtle. And she's not all that young anymore and has boobs like a swimming belt. I always listen in on conversations — that always interests me. You never know what you might learn from it. Of course I was right: they only just met. And he orders cigarettes at eight marks, when he usually only orders at four, I'm sure! The jerk. When they order those at eight, you know immediately what's on their minds. If a man is respectable, he only smokes those at six when he's with a lady, because that's the decent thing to do, and the change later on is less noticeable. I was once with an old fart who ordered at ten — what can I say, he was a sadist, and I would be embarrassed to put on paper what it was that he wanted from me. From me of all people, who can't tolerate even the slightest bit of pain. I already suffer immensely when my garters are too tight. I've been suspicious ever since.

Now I'm really stunned: the turtle orders Camembert! I have to ask myself: Is she really that innocent or is it that she doesn't want to? It's just so like me to have to think about everything. So here's what I'm thinking: if she doesn't want to, then eating Camembert is a safeguard for her, because she'll be inhibited by it. I'm thinking of my first date with Arthur Grönland. He was so good-looking and had style. But I said to myself: Doris, be strong — especially someone with style is ultimately impressed by respectability. And I really needed a wrist watch, and so it was better not to give in for the first three nights. But I know myself after all and I knew Arthur Grönland would order *Kupferberg* — and there was music too! So I attached seven rusty safety pins to my bra and my undershirt. I was stone drunk — like 80 naked savages — but I did not forget about the rusty safety pins. And Arthur Grönland kept pushing. And me: "But Sir, what are you thinking of me? I'm shocked. Who do you think I am?" And he was really impressed. Of course he was mad at first, but then, being a man of noble sentiment, he said that he liked a girl who was in control of herself even when she was soused. And he respected my lofty morals. I merely said: "It's my nature, Herr Grönland."

And when we came to my doorstep, he kissed my hand. I just said: "I still don't know what time it is — since my watch has been broken for so long." And I was thinking, if he just offers to give me the money to have it fixed, I will have been disappointed once again.

But the following night he arrived at the Rix Bar with a small golden one. I acted so surprised: "How on earth did you know that I needed a watch? But you're insulting me, I couldn't possibly. . . ."

So he turned all white and apologized and put the watch away. And I was trembling and thinking: "Now you went too far, Doris! So I said, with tears in my voice: "Herr Grönland, I can't bear to hurt you — please put it on for me."

So he thanked me and I said: "You're welcome." And then he thrust himself on me again, but I remained strong. And when we were at my front door, he said: "Please forgive me, you innocent creature, for having been so pushy."

And I said: "I forgive you, Herr Grönland."

But actually I was pretty mad at those safety pins, because he had the sweetest black eyes and such style, and the small gold watch was softly ticking away on my arm. But ultimately I'm too decent to let a man see that I have seven rusty safety pins stuck on my underwear. Later on, I would do without them.

Now it occurs to me that I too could eat Camembert whenever I feel I want to keep my reins on.

And the guy is squeezing the turtle's hand under the table, and he's staring at me with goggle eyes — that's men for you! And they have no idea that we see through them better than they see themselves. Of course I could — he's just starting to tell her about his wonderful motorboat on the Rhine with such and such horsepower — my guess is it's a high-end dinghy. And I can tell that he's talking at the top of his voice, so I can hear him — no wonder! I'm wearing my elegant hat and the coat with the fox collar, and the fact that I'm starting to write into my dove-covered notebook undoubtedly looks very intriguing. But just now the alligator smiles at me and that always softens me up. I'm thinking: there's hardly ever anything out there for you, you poor turtle — perhaps you're eating Camembert tonight but who knows about tomorrow? And I'm much too decent and too much into women's Lib to take your questionable balding boat owner away from you. It would just be too easy to do, so I'm not interested. Plus his water sports and her swim belt bosom make such a great combination. And there's a man with fabulously clean-cut features, like Conrad Veidt when he was at the height of his career, wearing a diamond ring on his pinky, who's looking at me from the other end of the room. Usually, there's not much behind faces like that. But I'm intrigued just the same.

I'm walking on air and I'm so excited. I just came home. I have a box of chocolates next to me — I'm eating them, but I only bite into those with the creamy filling to find out if they have nuts in them — if not, I don't like them — so I press them back together, so they will look like new — and tomorrow I'll give them to my mother and Therese. I received the box from the Conrad Veidt type — his name is Armin — actually I hate that name, because they once used it in a magazine commercial for a laxative.

And every time he got up from the table, I had to think: Armin, did you take *Laxin* this morning? And I had this idiotic laugh, and he would ask: "Why do you laugh this silvery laugh, you sweet creature?"

And me: "I'm laughing because I'm happy."

Thank God men are far too full of themselves to think that you could be laughing at them! And he told me he was an aristocrat. Well, I'm not so dumb to believe that live noblemen are running around in the streets these days. But I thought to myself: do him a favor, and so I said that I had been able to tell immediately. But he had an artistic touch and we had an exciting evening. We danced really well and had a good conversation. That's hard to come by these days. He did tell me that he wanted to get me into the movies — well, I pretended not to hear it. They just can't help themselves. It's a male sickness to tell every girl that they are the top executive of a film studio or at least that they have great connections. All I'm asking myself is if there are still any girls left who fall for that.

But none of that is really important now. What really matters is that I saw Hubert, just as he was leaving. And he has been gone for an entire year — God, I'm so tired now. Actually Hubert was pretty nasty, but I became kind of reserved with the laxative guy nonetheless. But he was only in town on business anyway. I'm sure Hubert didn't see me, but it still hit me like a bullet — his black coat from the back and his fair neck — and I had to think of our outing to the *Kuckuckswald*, where he lay on the ground with his eyes closed. And the sun made the ground hum and the air was trembling — and I put ants on his face while he was sleeping, because I'm never tired when I'm with a man I'm in love with — and I put ants in his ears — and Hubert's face was like a mountain range with valleys and all and he would pucker his nose in a funny way and his mouth was half open — his breath came out of it like a cloud. And he almost looked like a looney, but I loved him more for his sleepy face than for his kisses — and his kisses were quite something, let me tell you. And then he would call me "squirrel" because I have this way of pushing my lips up over my upper teeth — and I would always do that because he thought it was funny and it would make him happy. And he thought I didn't know I was doing it — and of course you let a man believe that.

So now I'm dog-tired and I wish I didn't have to take my dress off — when I was with Gustav Mooskopf, I got so tired once, I stayed over — just because I had a long way home and he could help me take my shoes off and whatnot — and here men always think it's love or sensuality or both — or because they have such great aura that makes you swoon and go wild — but what they don't know is that there are a million reasons for a girl to sleep with a guy. But none of that is important. Just quickly jotting down my thoughts, actually because I'm too tired to get up — thank God I'm wearing pumps and they're already under the table — I should put them on shoe trees because suede. . . .

I'm writing at the office, because the pimply face is in court. The girls are wondering what it is that I'm writing. Letters, I tell them — so they think it's got something to do with love, and they respect that. And Therese is eating my chocolates and is glad that I had another adventure. She's such a good sport, and since she herself doesn't have a life anymore because of her married guy, she partakes in my life. I love telling her about everything, because she has this great way of being surprised — even though it's always the same thing, really — but if I didn't have her to listen to me, I wouldn't feel like having such fabulous adventures.

I'm trying to figure out where it is that Hubert lives around here. Whether he's staying with family and that it would be best not to see him ever again. Because I started the relationship when I was 16 and he was my first, and very shy, despite the fact that he was in his late 20s already. And at first he didn't want to, not for moral reasons but because he was a coward, because he was thinking that he would be indebted to me, such an innocent girl. And I was innocent. But of course it never occurred to him that he was just a chicken but thought of himself as so noble, so he would have done anything except for that one thing. But I think getting a girl all worked up is the same thing as doing the other thing, and then I was thinking, there has to be a first time and it was important to me that it would be the real thing, and I was in love with him, with my head, my mouth, and further down. And then I got him to do it. But of course he thought he had seduced me and made a big to-do about his bad conscience, but he really wanted to have one and feel like he was a helluva guy — and you don't destroy that belief in a man. And we were together for an entire year and I was never with anyone else, because I didn't feel like it when I could only think about Hubert. And so I was what they call faithful. But then he finished his Ph.D. and was done with his studies, physics or something like that. And he went back to

Munich, where his parents lived, to get married — a woman of his standing, the daughter of a professor — very famous, but not as famous as Einstein, whose picture you see all over the newspapers and still don't have much of an idea. And every time I see a picture of him, with his cheerful eyes and his mobhead, I'm thinking if I ran into him in a café, wearing my coat with the fox collar and elegant from head to toe, perhaps he too would tell me that he was in the film industry and had incredible connections. And I would simply tell him: H_2O is water — that's what I learned from Hubert, and he would be stunned. But back to Hubert. So I didn't have a problem with him marrying for money and what have you — out of ambition, to get ahead — I always understand. Despite the fact that those canned sardines in his dumpy apartment tasted a lot better than any fancy schnitzel I had with Käsemann in a posh restaurant. As far as I'm concerned, sardines are good enough. But as I mentioned, I adjusted to Hubert's ambition. That's when he got really mean. First of all, he wanted to leave three days before my birthday — and he didn't even have a present for me. That had never been his thing, all he ever gave me was a little plastic frog that I would float down the river just for fun. I used to wear it on a velvet ribbon around my neck, under my blouse, that's how dedicated I was to him, even though the plastic legs dug into my neck — and I have very sensitive skin, as I mentioned. Which is an advantage — when you're dealing with men. But not when you have a sunburn. So he leaves three days before my birthday. I had to take that personally, because I had saved up for a polka dot dress that I was planning to wear on that day — for Hubert of course. And then I ended up all by myself in my new dress at a music bar with Therese. And I was crying my eyes out, and had to wipe my nose with my genuine suede gloves, because I didn't have a handkerchief, and Therese had a heavy cold. And my tears fell on my new dress — and all I needed was for the dots to run and ruin my salmon-colored outfit. But at least that didn't happen. That was one of the nasty things he did. The other one was that he shared this moral double standard with me. We're sitting in a restaurant, and all of a sudden he starts talking about that bitch from Munich. I just nod, still working on my emotional adjustment: he's got his reasons, I'm thinking, but he really loves only you.

So he gets all red in his face and embarrassed, and that already gets me up in arms. "When a man marries, he wants a virgin, and I hope, my little Doris . . ." and he was talking as if he had licked out an entire can of cold cream: "My dear child," he said, "I hope you'll become a decent girl, and as a man, I can only advise you not to sleep with a man until you're married to him. . . ."

I have no idea what else it was he wanted to say, because something came over me as he was blowing himself up, so impressed with himself, with his chest pushed out and his shoulders pulled back, like a general talking from the pulpit. To tell me that! To me who had seen him in his underwear and less almost 300 times — with his freckled belly and his hairy bow legs. At least he could have told me as a good friend that he wanted money and that's why he didn't want me. But to wallow in his own morality, not because I'm too poor but because I'm not decent enough, because I . . . well, I simply couldn't stand for that. In situations like that I just lose my mind and something comes over me. I can't really explain why I got so angry, suffice it to say that I slapped his face in front of all those people, which is something I do only rarely. And it made such a noise that the waiter thought I was asking for the check.

Right now I'm sitting in a restaurant. I've eaten enormous amounts of liverwurst, despite the fact that I could hardly get anything down, but it went down after all and I can only hope that it's not going to harm me, given how upset I am. Because I've been fired and I'm shaking like a leaf. And I'm terrified of having to go home. I've come to know my father as an extremely unpleasant man without any sense of humor, when he's at home. It's not at all unusual — men who're all Italian sunshine when they're with their buddies at the bar, and who've got a big mouth and are entertaining everybody — and at home with their families they are such sourpusses that looking at them after they've spent a night with the bottle is like eating a pickled herring.

And here is how it all happened: I hadn't been writing enough letters because I had been thinking about Hubert, and all of a sudden I had to go full steam ahead, to have something to show for by the end of the day. Of course there were no commas in sight, which is one of my strategies: because I figure, it's better to have no commas at all than commas in the wrong places, since it's easier to pencil them in than have to erase them. And there were still more mistakes in my letters and I had my doubts about them. So I put on my Marlene Dietrich face as I go into his office, like I'm making those big eyes at him like I can't wait to jump into bed with him. And the Pimple Face tells everyone to go home, only I have to stay and write those letters over again, which grosses me out, and I never feel like it, because they are files with some kind of nonsense about some guy Blasewitz, who had had a gold crown stolen by his dentist, who then charged him for it — I can't make any sense of it, and for weeks I've been writing about Blasewitz and his molars, which can really get on your nerves. So I go to see the Pimple Face — everybody has left already — it's only him and myself. And he's going over my letters, marking them with commas in ink — and I'm thinking to myself, What can you do? and casually brush against him, as if by accident. And he keeps putting in more and more commas, and crosses out words and corrects, and he's about to tell me that one of the letters has to be written again. But as he says "again" I press my breasts against his shoulder, and when he looks up I madly flare my nostrils, because I want to go home and don't want to write about Blasewitz's molars anymore and about Frau Gumpel's payments for that stinky old dairy store. And so I had to distract the Pimple Face and was flaring my nostrils like one of those giant Belgian rabbits when they eat cabbage. And just as I want to whisper that my poor old father has rheumatism and I've been reading "Happiness at the Gates" — just as I want to say it, it happens, and I notice too late that I've gone too far with those nostrils. So the guy jumps up and clutches me and breathes heavily like a locomotive about to leave the station. And I say: but — and I try to get his disgusting bony fingers off of me, and I'm really confused, because I hadn't expected all of this for another four weeks, and this just goes to show you that you always learn something new. And he says: "My child, stop pretending. I've know for a long time that you have feelings for me and that your blood longs for me."

Well, all I can say is that it beats me how a man who has a degree and who is able to follow all that stuff about Blasewitz and his molars, how a man like that can be so stupid. And it was Hubert's fault and my empty stomach and everything happened so quickly and the pimples and he was moving his mouth like a flounder — so I lost control of the situation. And I whisper nonsense — the usual stuff — and he wants to push me over toward the cold leather sofa — and I haven't even had dinner yet, and might have to rewrite those letters after all — I wouldn't put it beyond him, being an attorney — so I figured, enough of it. So I said very calmly: "How dare you wrinkle my dress like this, when I don't have anything to wear already!" And that was a hint and a test, and whether I would rebuff him gently and politely or get mean all depended on his response. Naturally, I got just the answer I had expected: "My child, how can you think about this now, and I like you best naked and without any clothes on anyway."

That really blew my mind. I kicked his shin so he would let go of me and said: "Now tell me one thing, you stupid attorney, what on earth are you thinking? How can a highly educated man like yourself be so dumb to think that a pretty young girl like myself would be crazy about him? Have you ever looked at yourself in the mirror? I'm asking you, what sex appeal could you possibly have?"

It would have been very interesting to hear a logical response, because a man has to be thinking something after all. But instead he just said: "So that's the kind you are!"

And he draws out the "that" as if it were *gum arabica*. And so I go: "That kind or not that kind — I consider it a wonder of nature to see you turn blue in the face with anger, and I never would have thought that you could get even meaner than you already are — and your wife dyes her hair yellow like egg yolks and is into expensive cosmetics and cruising around in her car all day and doing nothing in terms of honest work — and I'm supposed to do it with you for nothing, just for love. And I slap his pimply face with that letter about Blasewitz and his molars; since I had nothing more to lose, at least I wanted to give my temperament full rein. Of course he gave me notice effective the first of the month. I just said: "I've also had it with you. Just give me one month's salary and I won't be back again."

And I made cheeky threats — that the guys in court would only have to look at his miserable face and would believe me immediately that I had never given him any sensual looks and I would win my case — or if he wanted me to tell the girls in the office tomorrow, particularly since he used vulgar words like naked and that my blood was longing for him. And when I get really excited about something, I just have to tell somebody. And now I'm sitting here with my 120 marks and am trying to figure out my future. And I'm waiting for Therese, whom I called, so she can come and comfort me and calm me down, since after all, I've just lived through a sensational event.

I told my mother everything, but only mentioned 60 marks of which I kept 20 which makes a total of 80 for myself. Because you have to appreciate money, and you learn that when you're working. And I have to hand it to my mother; she's quite a woman. She still has a certain something from the old days, even though she's working the cloakroom at the theater these days. She may be a bit overweight, but not too bad and she wears her hats in an old-fashioned kind of way — kind of like a dot on the i — but that's becoming fashionable again. In any case, she carries herself like a really expensive lady, and that's because she used to have a life. Unfortunately, she married my father, which was a mistake, I think, because he's completely uneducated and as lazy as a dead body and only shouts every once in a while to show off his big mouth — we all know about that sort of thing. Only when he's not at home does he have manners, including elegant gestures with his arms, pulling up his eyebrows, and wiping the sweat off his forehead — particularly in the company of women who weigh more than 500 pounds and aren't married to him.

To make a long story short, I don't have much of an opinion of the man and the only reason I'm scared now is because my nerves can't take it when he loses his temper — and when he talks to me about morals, I can't really do anything about it because he is my father. And I've been asking my mother why she as a high-class woman settled for this loser, and instead of slapping me she just said: "You have to belong somewhere after a while." And she was completely calm — but I almost cried, and don't know why, but I understood and never complained about the old curmudgeon ever again.

I would just love to see Hubert again. And I can feel that great things are in store for me. But at this point, I'm still sitting here with 80 marks and without a new source of income and I ask you, Where is my man for this emergency? Times are horrible. Nobody has any money and there is an immoral spirit in the air — just as you're getting ready to hit on someone for some cash, they're already hitting on you!

So Therese advised me to check out Johnny Klotz, a fellow we know at the ice cream parlor — that's because he's got a car — nothing special, but it's something. And me: "You don't know about men nowadays, Therese — what do you mean a man with a car, when it's not paid off? If you have money nowadays, you go by streetcar and to have 25 pfennigs in cash is worth more than owning a car on credit." Therese understood, because she accepts my authority when it comes to things like this. So I'm racking my brain as to how I might be able to get back on my feet, because when you rely on men completely, things are bound to go wrong. Unless it's someone really big — and that's hard to come by in a crummy town like this. In any case, Johnny Klotz is going to teach me the new tango tonight, so I'll stay on top of things. I'm so fidgety — sitting around all day with nothing to do. I'm dying for it to get dark, and I constantly have that melody in my ears: I love you, my brown madonna — sunshine is glowing in your eyes. . . . And the violinist at the *Palastdiele* has a voice like sugar — oh my God — and I have to swallow whole that kind of night with music and lights and dancing, until I've had my fill — as if I were going to be dead by tomorrow morning and were never ever to get anything again. I want to have a pale pink tulle dress with silver lace and a ruby red rose pinned at my shoulder — I'm going to try to land a job as a model, I'm a gold star — and silver shoes . . . oh what a tango fairy tale . . . and what wonderful music there is — when you're drunk, it's like going down a slide.

There has been a significant development in my life, as I am now an artist. It all started out with my mother talking to Frau Buschmann who runs the cloakroom for the actresses, and she in turn spoke with Frau Baumann, who plays old and funny ladies — those crazy old women who still want to, but no one wants them any more, and people find that funny, but there's really nothing funny about it. And she spoke to someone by the name of Klinkfeld who directs plays and is called director. And Klinkfeld spoke to someone who is one notch below him and directs plays under him. His name is Bloch and he is a stage manager and has a tummy like a throw pillow — I'm not sure if it's embroidered or not — and he always pretends to be incredibly excited as if the theater belonged to him and is running around with a book in his hand saying vulgar things, and you never know if it's in the book or if these are his own words. And Bloch spoke with the box opener who stands in front of the director's box that provides direct access from the auditorium to the stage — which is prohibited and the box opener stands there with an impressive posture to make sure nobody steals the props. And he spoke with my mother and now I'm an extra. And I have to run across the stage in a play called *Wallenstein's Camp* holding a jug together with other girls — it's quite a scene — but it's just a rehearsal for the time being, and the performance isn't until the 12th. Until then it's supposed to get even wilder. And nobody talks to me, because they all think they're something special.

The girls are made up of two halves — one half is with the conservatory and only participates for money and feels like God's gift to the world, and the others are with the drama school. They don't get paid, but pay for it — and feel like a million dollars. The same thing is true for the male extras. And they carry on in a way that I've never seen before in my life and treat me with condescension, which they are going to regret. And the real actors look down on those from the drama school and are sure to let them know. They also look down on each other, but that they don't show too much. In any case, there's a hell of a lot of looking down on each other, and everyone thinks they're the only one who's wonderful. And the janitors are the only ones who act like normal people and greet you when you say hello to them.

Downstairs there's a small room where the actors sit when they don't have to be on stage, and the whole space is filled with smoke and you can hardly breathe. And everyone talks in an affected kind of voice and listens to himself, because no one else is listening. Except when someone is telling a joke, because that's something they can tell the next person right away, with their affected voices. And they keep running back and forth and have strong upper thighs and then they stop all of a sudden and stare at a piece of paper in a frame that is called rehearsal schedule. And then they jiggle their feet and hum interesting tunes, despite the fact that no one is looking. Only sometimes people from the outside stop by and they get all excited and breathe heavily. And the less important actors mooch cigarettes from each other. And sometimes they give some to each other too.

And then every morning the director comes in from the street. That's a very solemn moment. You can tell by the way he pulls the door open that he rules over the theater. And because he's a big fish and thinks highly of himself, he is almost always thin-lipped and in a bad mood. Otherwise he's kind of chubby and has greenish skin and his name is Leo Olmütz. And he always sticks his head into the porter's window really quickly and then pulls it right back — I have no idea why — but it has a great effect. And then he walks down the hallway to his office with those hard soles. The girls from the school make sure he notices them, whenever they intentionally happen to bump into him. And today he said to two of them: "Hello, girls — looks like you're in a great mood." That was sensational and they talked about it until noon. The fat blonde, whose face is shiny with grease and red as a tomato and who is called Linni, claims he had given her this look. And the other one with the black pageboy and her filthy mouth who is called Pilli said no. And then still others joined in, and later on they argued whether he had said "hey" or not. And they all formed a gang and looked at me condescendingly, because I wasn't supposed to hear what they were whispering — and I was sitting nearby at the table in what is called the conversation lounge.

And all of a sudden, I said very calmly: "I'd be happy to ask Leo tonight whether he said 'hey' or not."

Everybody was staring at me. I noticed immediately that I was on the right track to get them to respect me.

That thin drip of a girl Pilli just asked: "So do you know him?"

And me: "Know who? Leo? Well, of course. He's personally in charge of my training here, but he doesn't want me to talk about it. And besides, I'm supposed to keep my distance from all the goings-on around here."

And I arrogantly wrinkled my nose and glanced dreamily through the top window. After that they're swarming around me like bumblebees, and that fatso Linni invites me right away to have coffee with her after rehearsal. I'm quietly eating five pieces of danish, thinking to myself: let her pay while I'm getting the inside story on this outfit. Of course, I avoid talking about Leo, since after all I don't know the first thing about him, and I get off the subject as soon as she asks and admit to nothing. Afterward we cross the street — and I can tell she doubts me — and so I stop in front of a fabric store, make an impressive gesture, and casually remark: "Leo had three pairs of pajamas made from this lovely fabric."

And Linni, full of awe: "The crêpe de chine with the floral pattern?"

I hadn't realized I had pointed at the floral pattern — and now all I could do was nod and pretend I had a coughing fit, because I was dying with laughter picturing that thin-lipped blob with his important heavy step wearing pajamas of white crepe de chine with little roses on it. And I thought to myself that I owed her an explanation, so as soon as I had regained control over myself, I said: "Yes, he did that for my sake. I asked him because I just love that fabric and I think it just makes for a splendid contrast with his dark hair."

Even though he's hardly got any hair left.

Then I swore her to secrecy. And now I'm terrified that someone will say something. And I'm scared because of how that's going to make me look when the truth comes out — and to tell you the truth, I'm already sick and tired of the theater.

Art is something lofty, and I'm suffering for it and already had a success. So I found out that the drama students are more important than those who just participate. And so I'm thinking to myself, I'm not going to stay with the riffraff. And the more you get to say on stage, the more important you are, and it's all about being listed on that piece of paper, and to get on it, you have to say something. So there was all this commotion about one sentence in that play called *Wallenstein's Camp*. There's this old woman who sleeps with a lot of soldiers. They don't tell you that, but it's obvious. And she also sells food to the soldiers, but I'm thinking to myself that that doesn't pay the bills, particularly when there's been a war on for 30 years. And this old woman has a relative who is young, and of course she also sleeps with the soldiers because what else is she going to do after all. And she's called *vivandrière*, which is a foreign word — I would have loved to ask the girls about it. But despite my story with Leo I hesitate to demonstrate my ignorance, which is never a good idea, by the way. Because you only get oppressed. And because those two females that are called vivandrières have such energy — I'm thinking it must have something to do with being vivacious. And this just goes to show you that a little thought can help you explain many things to yourself, and that you don't have to ask. And the younger vivandrière is running around and pouring drinks and is sitting in a tent, which isn't there yet — not until the dress rehearsal. And she comes out of the tent once and shouts: "Aunt, they're off!" Referring to the soldiers of course. And she has to sound very excited, which makes no sense to me, because there's still plenty of them staying behind and one more or less doesn't seem to make a difference — especially with soldiers who are a dime a dozen anyway. And at first Klinkfeld was going to cut the role of the young vivandrière, since she would only be detracting from the military. But now he's changed his mind and she's supposed to say one sentence. And that one sentence caused as much of a stir as a loaf of bread during a famine. If not more so.

Because it was only one sentence, the real actresses weren't keen on the role. So one of the girls from the drama school was supposed to get it. And there are seven of them, and in October, after the auditions for the new students, there will be still more. All of them have to train for two years. Beats me what there is to learn, but I'll stay out of that for now and keep my mouth shut, since I'm with the school too now, and I also have a success.

But back to the sentence. That fatso Linni was after me to talk to Leo so she would get to say the sentence. That was embarrassing, and all I could tell her is that Leo would not feel like hearing anything about sentences after a hard day's work — plus he's so passionate, he won't be able to think of anything else.

So then she wants to know more about Leo's erotic style. Just goes to show you what those artsy girls are like — no different from those at the office or anywhere else. They always want to hear details. I've really had it with all those questions about Leo. Whenever I see him coming down the hallway, I feel a knot in my stomach and I get weak and dizzy.

And all I say to Linni is: "Leo doesn't appreciate my talking about his sex life."

And Pilli, that flat-chested bag of bones, is constantly hanging out in front of the directors' office just to hit on Klinkfeld, which I figured out right away. So all the girls got into a fight, and then they made up, and then they got into a fight again — I guess, if you have nothing better to do. . . . And Manna Rapallo, that short little button, started up a relationship with Bloch, who is called a stage manager, and who's constantly running around with a big tummy and a book in his hands — only so he would get her the sentence. But what is most interesting to me is that these are all girls with a higher education and they are crazy about saying the sentence of a vivandrière who's clearly from the proletariat. And that just goes to show you that theater has absolutely nothing to do with real life.

So today Klinkfeld says during rehearsal: "Oh my God, there's still that sentence."

And although he usually has a rather nervous voice and is jumping up and down like a kangaroo, he says this with complete nonchalance and to top everything off, he runs his hand across his head, which seems to be a particular habit of men who don't have any hair that could be out of place. And then they get in a bad mood, because they've made the unpleasant discovery that it's all smooth up there. Käsemann used to do that too, and I couldn't get him to stop.

So as soon as Klinkfeld mentions that sentence, all of the girls are throbbing like one single heart — except for me. And they all had to say it and potbellied Bloch pushed that little button Manno Rapallo to the front of the line and said loudly — to pay her back for having her — "She's never had a sentence before. All the others have had one already." And so she too had to say the sentence, but unfortunately all that excitement with the potbelly had gotten to her, and so she sounded like a hooded crow. And then Mila von Trapper got the sentence. Just imagine, a real aristocrat with a former general for a father playing a proletarian vivandrière. All I can say is that theater is incredibly interesting. Mila von Trapper has Chinese eyes and a great figure, I have to admit. But her meanness toward me is beyond belief, since she didn't come to rehearsals until later and has no idea about me and Leo. She's very proud because she has a lot of talent, which means a lot around here. To have no talent is worse than being in jail. And Mila von Trapper once made talent in the conversation room, after everyone had already left — only the girls from the school were still there, those who would love to spend the night at the theater. They were all sitting on the table and on the window sill, making solemn faces and serious mouths, and proud Trapper was making talent and was screaming. Something vulgar about Holofernes and that she wouldn't give him a son, which nobody has asked her to do anyway. Anyhow, the kind of stuff you find in difficult plays. And so she was rolling around on the floor in agony, like Aunt Clara when she has kidney stones — and she was screaming her guts out. I didn't like it, I have to say, but I couldn't scream that loud. And then she pretended she was cutting someone's head off with a sword. She was waving her arms as if it was difficult to get his head to come off. I thought that was a bit brutal. And she was screaming and going on like mad. Very scary. And apparently, the whole thing is called an outburst. And everyone thought it was just great, a perfect audition piece.

And since I couldn't think of anything profound to say, but she had made such an effort and was completely out of breath, I wanted to say something nice too. So when she cast these questioning looks at me, I said: "Just be careful not to get into a draft right now. You've gotten really hot with all that screaming, and the flu is going around."

So she makes this horrible face at me, which sent shivers down my back, and says: "Apparently, this work of art made no impression on you at all. Perhaps you don't even know who wrote *Judith* — anything's possible."

Of course it is possible that I don't know who Judith is, maybe it's the name of the play she was shouting. For a short while I felt surrounded by a cloud of sadness. I constantly find myself in situations where I don't know something and I have to pretend that I do, and constantly having to pay attention makes me really tired sometimes. And I'm always supposed to feel ashamed when words come up that I don't know, and people are never good to me so I would have the courage to tell them: "I know I'm stupid but I have a good memory, and when you explain something to me, I make every effort to remember it."

And without meaning to, I heard these words coming out of my mouth: "No, I don't know who she is." Because there are moments when I'm just dying not to have to lie. But you pay for that, of course.

So Trapper says to me: "Unfortunately, art is becoming more and more proletarian." And I could tell by looking at her neck that she had said something nasty to me.

But then Linni took her aside and told her about me and Leo. So she immediately turned as sweet as honey. But I was mad at myself because I had shown my weakness. How am I going to get through life like that?

So yesterday, the Trapper got the sentence, since she has a talent for outbursts. But I hate her — Why did she have to be so mean to me? That's the last outburst she's had for a while!

This morning I saw Trapper make her way up to the second floor in her high heels. It was only moments before she had to say the sentence — so I followed her. She disappears in the bathroom stall. God must have been with me — because the key was stuck outside! I turn it, very quietly, and run off. Nobody sees me. Let her scream her head off in there. It would have to be quite a coincidence for anyone to be going upstairs. There's another bathroom downstairs, which everyone else uses. But our aristocratic Trapper always has to have something special. Now she's got it.

So the sentence didn't get said, and Klinkfeld was about to throw a fit, because it was holding up the rehearsal. So I dash out of the tent, which isn't there yet — I was wearing my tight, bright red gown — and scream at the top of my lungs: "Cousin, they're off!"

And since I was genuinely terrified, my voice got all heavy with sorrow about the soldiers that are leaving.

So Klinkfeld pulls his hand over his bald spot and asks me who I am.

I tell him. So he gets mad at the aristocrat who's not there and says: "You can have the sentence."

And all the girls hated me. That's why they're in awe about me. So after the rehearsal I go down to the office and as I walk back and forth, I hear the Trapper pounding against the bathroom door. But that wasn't doing her any good, because right above her, workers were hammering together the stage decorations and were making an incredible racket that the aristocrat had no chance of overpowering. And I run up to Klinkfeld and make him swear on his word of honor and as the director of the play that I can keep the sentence, even though I'm not a student at the school. So he talks to me and seems very interested, completely without desire, which I think was because he hadn't had his lunch yet. So he asks me to come into his office and has me sit down in the easy chair, so he has only the regular chair to sit on. I'll never forget that, because that was true elegance on his part, since, after all, he didn't want anything from me.

And then he goes next door — to Leo — and they both come out. I'm facing Leo and turn bright red and my face starts to twitch, because in my mind he's wearing those white crepe-de-chine pajamas, and it's almost vulgar to be imagining that. And at the same time, he's surrounded by this aura of dignity. With the sun in their faces, they looked like little red Chinese lanterns. And with his thin-lipped smile he inadvertently looked like the Mona Lisa. My knees were like ice and I felt like I had a boulder in my stomach. Because important men without erotic desire, which gives you an advantage over them, really impress me. So they asked me all sorts of questions about my educational background and what I wanted.

And then they asked me to audition for them, and I recited the *Erlkönig*. But when I got to "mit Kron' und Schweif" I couldn't remember the words anymore, which was truly embarrassing. So they asked me to present something comical, and we all thought long and hard about it. Finally, I did that song about Elizabeth and her beautiful legs, and I danced to it.

So they laughed and Klinkfeld said to Leo:

"She's a natural comedienne."

And Leo nodded his head and said: "And she's very graceful too."

All the while I was standing there looking at my shoes and pretending not to hear. But of course I heard every single word they said. And they accepted me into the school, and I don't have to pay for it, they were going to see to that. So I'm no longer at the bottom of the totem pole.

But at the same time, there's a lot of friction at home. My father is yelling and screaming about how I'm going to make a living now, and my mother wants this career for me, and I can hardly eat anything anymore because of all that ado. My father is an old man and his life consists only of filthy cards and drinking beer and schnapps, and sitting around in bars — and that costs money! So when I no longer give him anything, I'm actually taking away from him. And I don't cost him any money, except for sleeping in that crummy attic — and I hardly ever eat at home, but get invited to eat out. But now his entire face spells reproach. Looks like I'm going to have to find me a man to pay for my clothes and 50 marks a month for at home, so he keeps quiet. And if I tell him how I got the money, he kicks me out — for moral reasons. But if I don't tell him, he doesn't ask and doesn't wonder about it, because he gets the money and it gives him peace of mind when he doesn't have to think about anything.

And one woman was singing and wiggling her bosoms — wearing a yellow dress with a rose on the shoulder and a ton of blue paint on her eyes. And another man was riding a bicycle — a really high one — and was cracking jokes, risking his life — and people are eating, and you're sweating like a pig — and then they clap. He could have been dead — how much do they pay a guy like that? It was first-rate cabaret.

An industrialist had invited me along. He had come to the theater to pick up free tickets for tomorrow night, because if you have money you have connections, and then you don't have to pay. You can really live on the cheap, if you're rich. So he talked to me and invited me, because he took me for an established artist. I want to become one. I want to become a star. I want to be at the top. With a white car and bubble bath that smells from perfume, and everything just like in Paris. And people have a great deal of respect for me because I'm glamorous, and they'll find it so cute when I don't know what "capacity" means and won't laugh at me like they do now — just wondering if the Trapper is still locked in the bathroom. If I haven't seen her by tomorrow, I'll go upstairs and unlock the door, because I don't really want her to starve to death.

I'm going to be a star, and then everything I do will be right — I'll never have to be careful about what I do or say. I don't have to calculate my words or my actions — I can just be drunk — nothing can happen to me anymore, no loss, no disdain, because I'm a star.

The industrialist dropped me already. And it's all because of politics. Politics poisons human relationships. I spit on it. The emcee was a Jew, the one on the bike was a Jew, the one who was dancing was a Jew. . . .

So he asks me if I'm Jewish too. My God, I'm not — but I'm thinking: if that's what he likes, I'll do him the favor — and I say: "Of course — my father just sprained his ankle at the synagogue last week."

So he says, he should have known, with my curly hair. Of course it's permed, and naturally straight like a match. So he gets all icy; turns out he's nationalist with a race, and race is an issue — and he got all hostile — it's all very difficult. So I did exactly the wrong thing. But

I didn't feel like taking it all back. After all, a man should know in advance whether he likes a woman or not. So stupid! At first they pay you all sorts of compliments and are drooling all over you — and then you tell them: I'm a chestnut! — and their chin drops: oh, you're a chestnut — yuk, I had no idea. And you are exactly the way you were before, but just one word has supposedly changed you.

I'm drunk. Wondering if Hubert is still in town. Once the industrialist was soused, he wasn't so principled anymore, and wanted to. And when I told him that my hair was naturally straight, he turned me into a race with blood and really went at it. But I had lost interest, because once he's sober again, he'll start all over again with politics, and you never know if you won't get yourself assassinated for political reasons, if you get involved.

At the table next to me was a wonderful lady with really expensive shoulders and with a back — it was straight all by itself, and such a wonderful dress, it makes me cry — the dress was so beautiful, because she doesn't have to think about where she's getting it from. You could tell by looking at the dress. And I was standing next to her in the restroom, and both of us were looking in the mirror — she had such light white hands with elegantly curved fingers and an assertive look on her face, and next to her I looked so labored. She was tall and not at all slender, and her hair was shiny and blonde. It must be interesting for a man to kiss her, because there's no way he would know in advance what it would be like. With me, they always know. I would have loved to have told her how beautiful she was and that I thought she looked like an evening song, but then she would have thought I was queer, and that would have been wrong.

Everything was covered in red velvet, and one woman was dancing under the headlights, but she also looked labored and really had to struggle. I'm wondering if you can become glamorous if you weren't born that way. But I'm already at the drama school. Still I don't have an evening coat — everything is half-baked — the thing with the fox is fine for the afternoon, but at night it's a piece of shit. The woman had a cape — black with white seal trim, could have been ermine. But she had an innate poise that would have made white rabbit look like ermine — that's like a sacred word to me and I'm getting goosebumps just thinking of it. When Therese is wearing genuine suede gloves, on her they still look like cloth.

I took the tram to get to the Cabaret, past the cemeteries. A woman got on who had just buried her husband — she was wearing a cloud of black veil, all in black she was, but no money for a taxi, black gloves, and everyone could see her face, her eyes were all kaput and she couldn't cry anymore — and she was wearing all black but carrying a little bright-red suitcase that was completely out of

style and small and bright red — and that gave me a stab-
bing pain in my heart — the shiny blonde, too. Once
again, I feel something spectacular in me, but it's painful
somehow.

Today was dress rehearsal — the tent is there too.
Leo was sitting in the dress circle, right next to Klinkfeld
and other exciting dignitaries from the city. I'm feeling
nauseous. I fear for my career and am ready to pass out,
because by now the entire theater knows of me and Leo.
Possibly, he's the only one who doesn't know yet that he's
having an affair with me. But how much longer can that
last? He's going to find out, the story about the pajamas
too, which is being told as an intimate joke at the theater now. I feel sick to my stomach. And then the rehearsal with all that noise and those loud decorations and
terribly colorful military. And I secretly stomped on that
monk's foot, the one that's giving a speech on a wooden
wagon, while the curtain was up, so he couldn't say anything. And that's because he's pinched me all day yesterday and the days before, in the dark behind the stage.
Others did it too, but the monk was the worst. What a
pig. And I've noticed that it's only the lowly actors, who
have very little to say, who pinch you and slap you on
the behind — why should I put up with that? I wouldn't
have said anything with the big ones, after all, they can
use a little distraction after all those endless sentences

and all that heavy screaming — and that's why it wouldn't have been so insulting to me, coming from them. Only the old farts and the lowlifes. And the monk had been pinching me more times than he had sentences and he was a royal pain in the ass.

But by this morning, everyone knew about me and Leo — and nobody was pinching me anymore. They only kept their distance, and used a lot of fancy language when speaking with me. Even the monk. But still I couldn't resist my opportunity for revenge on stage, and so I stepped on his foot with a vengeance, because I could tell by his filthy face that he had corns.

And the thing with Leo has been spreading because of the Trapper, because I have her sentence and I won't give it up. And so she's going all the way to the top. That's the kind she is. Thank God she has no idea that I locked her in the bathroom. There had been a lot of excitement because of that, since she had spent the night in there and was discovered by Wallenstein himself the next morning. And she had a nervous breakdown, which I've always felt was a made-up illness. And her father, who is a general, wants to use his connections to have a theater closed down where honest girls are locked in the bathroom. And the thing is taking its course. And so is the Trapper. At the rehearsal, that is. And she wants her sentence back. But Klinkfeld promised her an enormously long sentence in the next play. Instead of shutting up about it, she's getting everybody jealous by telling them about Leo and me. And she's insinuating that Leo himself locked her in the bathroom, as a turn-on for me. I find it utterly tasteless to drag such an elegant man into the mud like that. And the girls say that they can tell Leo is completely captivated by me, just by the way he walks past me. But he doesn't even look at me — I tell them that — but all they say is: "That's exactly why!" I feel sick to my stomach. This can't last much longer.

I'll be meeting Therese later. There's something soothing about her, after all this noise and excitement. Everybody wanting so much and at such volume, and Therese is someone who doesn't want anything — that's such a godsend. I'm going to give her my wooden pearl necklace with the yellow specks on it — that will give her some quiet pleasure.

Today we also put on make-up. It looked all waxy, under the lamps in the dressing rooms and the light that was coming through the window. And Linni looked like a puffed-up painted dead body, with eyes like burnt sunnyside-up eggs, and the Trapper looked as if she had been a hooker for years. I really had to watch closely to see how they do it, the eyeliner and all that, and my face became strange to me in an interesting way. And when I smiled at myself in the mirror, it looked like I had a slit in my face. I'm all for powder and lip gloss — Coty dark in particular — but I think it's wrong to do your make-up in a way that your own smile doesn't belong to your face anymore.

But on stage with the lighting it looked just right. And we were wearing gigantic hats made from cheap material, because it's the Thirty Years War — with huge feathers. I picked a hat with a white feather, because that's something you can reuse. After the play is taken off the program, I'll take it home. The rest of the costume is junk. It's all ripped, just like the things Frau Ellmann from next door wears when she goes to clean at fancy homes. That's so the lady of the house should feel the urge to give her clothes. And when she gets home she complains about them, like she doesn't wear that kind of crap — and uses them as rags to clean her apartment. And Frau Becker, who lives above her and whose husband makes her more babies than he makes money, she would be happy if someone gave her a ripped blouse. But no one gives her anything, because she's unassuming and decent. I hate the Ellmanns, for more than one reason.

What a day! It was the opening night of *Wallenstein*. I got more flowers than all the other actresses combined. That's because I had spread the word that I would be playing, and except for Hubert, all the men I had ever had a relationship with were at the theater. I had no idea there were so many! Except for them, the theater was empty. There was hardly anyone there.

Käsemann behaved very well, sending a basket filled with roses and a golden bow and in red letters: "Bravo to the young artist!"

So I'm almost a star now. And Gustav Mooskopf sent yellow chrysanthemums the size of my mother's head after she's had it done. And delicatessen owner Prengel brought a basket filled with sardines and tomato paste and the finest saveloy and a note that I shouldn't tell his wife. Only over my dead body. I wouldn't put it past that woman to use vitriol, that's why I'm staying away from Prengel whom I'd otherwise consider. And Johnny Klotz sent the horn from the Ford he's paying off, together with a note saying that unfortunately he once again didn't have a cent for flowers but he invites me and Therese to the *Mazurka-Bar* after the performance. He knows a waiter there who will take a rain check. And Jakob Schneider sent three elegant boxes of chocolate with purple ribbon and a yellow georgina and a polite invitation to have dinner with him at the *Schlossdiele*. But I can't do that because unfortunately, he's so cross-eyed that I start to get cross-eyed myself when I sit opposite him — and that makes me look less attractive, which is something that can't be expected of me.

And finally all I did was have a simple beer with Therese and Hermann Zimmer in a bar nearby. Because Hermann Zimmer is leaving on montage and he moved me by giving me a bouquet of asters — and he hardly has any money and is an old friend of mine. And he's a member of the Athlete's Club of which I'm the honorary lady member. And all the guys from the club sent a huge laurel and fir wreath decorated with colorful silk paper ornaments that was meant for the mayor's funeral last week, but then didn't get picked up because they couldn't pay for it — and that's why they got it cheaper. A beautiful piece that's going to last. And that made me indebted to them of course, because the whole Athlete's Club was joining us at the bar and there was a huge party. And all these guys had been sitting in the gallery and after my sentence they were shouting bravo, and Hermann Zimmer was stomping his feet, and Käsemann applauded from the dress circle and Gustav Mooskopf in his box was moving his chair back and forth in recognition. All of that got some other people to start hissing and whistling and Klinkfeld was shaking behind the set, because he thought they were communists and there would be a scandal at the theater. But it was because of me. I thought it better not to say anything, despite the fact that the Athlete's Club is convinced that I'm *the* attraction of the local theater.

I was dancing on the table, singing the song of Elizabeth and her beautiful legs — and they told me they liked that better than the entire Schiller. And Therese was drunk — I gave Hermann Zimmer some of Prengel's saveloy, so he would kiss her hand every five minutes and tell her some nice things, that she's looking beautiful and all that — because that's the kind of thing a woman wants to hear when she's soused. And she really developed some verve and if she finally forgets about that married guy of hers, perhaps she'll have a second flowering — it happens, and I would be very happy for her.

Perhaps I'll ask her tomorrow to call Hubert's relatives. Now that I'm famous and a star, I don't think he can hurt me any more. Perhaps I'll get written up in the papers tomorrow in a review. And then we all went over to the *Mazurka-Bar* to Johnny Klotz. It was terrific!

On the road, we were honking that interesting Ford horn, sounding like a Kaiser Wilhelm-Memorial Church — and people were running off in all directions and one guy was singing "Heil dir im Siegerkranz," he was drunk. We got to talking with him, due to a bottle of *Asbach* we had on us — we were taking turns with the bottle. The *Siegerkranz* type took pretty big gulps and had a broken look in his eyes. He told us that he had just pawned his Iron Cross for the 17th time at a bar, so he could go on drinking, and this way a life-threatening mission was finally becoming worth something, though not much. And we took him along to Johnny. He had a bald spot because of the steel helmet, but they all tell you that, unless they're under 30. And he said his life was over and that's why things were just starting to get interesting. The Athlete's Club was singing the *Marseillaise*, which is French, and he said this was giving him a new perspective. There was such hopelessness in the corners of his mouth, so I showered him with kisses because I felt sorry for him, which easily happens to me whenever I'm hammered.

And Therese was carrying a whole folder full of letters for the Pimple Face — that all seems so far away — Did I really used to work there? My life is moving at the speed of a bicycle race. So the letters had to be mailed and didn't have postage on them yet, and the stamps were beginning to stick to the folder. I understood that they had to be mailed. They were making me nervous and so Therese took them out of the folder, drunk as she was — and we wetted them with Cherry Cobler, since Johnny had licked the glue off of three of them, so you couldn't use them any more. And Therese went across the street to the mailbox, and got lost for half an hour. She has no sense of direction — when she goes to the bathroom in a restaurant, you need to give her a compass. And three of the guys lifted up one of the tables, all the way up — with Johnny's 200-pound waiter and myself on top. A tremendous achievement that can only be explained through enthusiasm and constant training. It was great!

So we were roaming the streets, singing songs without any politics, because that's the way I wanted it. *Das Wandern ist des Müllers Lust* and *Kommt ein Vogel geflogen*, which are so harmless that I have my doubts whether there isn't some secret meaning hidden in them.

And a cop wanted to give us a ticket, so the entire Athlete's Club offered him *Asbach*, but he didn't go for that. So I gave him this look — with my eyes and kissed one of the buttons on his uniform, and it got all foggy. And so did the cop. He didn't cite us.

I'm so feverish and full of excitement. Oh Hubert. And I'm surrounded by roses and a ton of flowers. I hung the laurel wreath over my bed, right where the Holy Thusnelda used to be with her fat arms, but I feel closer to the wreath. And on my night table, which is so shabby-looking — I bought it from the Beckers, because she really needed the money — despite the fact that it looks like a bad marriage — on that table is Käsemann's basket of roses with the bow flowing down onto my pillow. I'm going to put my face on top of it and go to sleep against the red letters: "Bravo to the young artist!" And unfortunately, I'm once again alone in bed.

If the doorbell rings, I'll go crazy. Dear God, please help me. This is the end of my stardom. It's all over — but for me that means it's just beginning. My heart is a gramophone playing inside of me, scratching my bosom with a sharp needle. Of course I don't have a bosom, because it smacks of the ordinary, like breastfeeding or an old opera diva where you can't tell what's bigger, her breasts or her voice. I'm writing in a fever and my hand is trembling. I'm trying to fill up the hours sitting in Therese's furnished room, which she never uses. It's always like that. What you have, you don't need, and what you need, you don't have. Dear God, my letters are trembling on the paper like the legs of dying mosquitoes. I have to stop.

Tonight I'm off to Berlin. You can go underground there, and Therese has a girlfriend there, where I can stay. I want to cry. But there's a desire in me that has gotten me to this point. My head is like an oven heated with coal. I could be arrested any minute — because of the fur coat, because of the Ellmanns, because of Leo and a cop or Trapper's general. . . . And all that because of Hubert and this feeling in my stomach that's totally foreign to me.

It was last night — another *Wallenstein*. I arrive at the theater to put on my make-up, and Therese is there waiting for me — she was done at the office and I was just starting. So she says: "Doris, Hubert called." He had asked about me, called up the Pimple-Face and Therese got on and set up a date at *Küppers Café* at eight, after the performance.

And it had to be that night that I was wearing my old raincoat — which happens about once a year — not so much because of rain, but because I needed sleep and wanted to go straight home, knowing my weakness for evening activities. And so I put on my disgusting coat that I wouldn't wear to go anywhere.

I love Therese. She's fabulous. As soon as I'm a star, I will shine on her and make her my sidekick. I'm scared.

Wondering if they take away your powder puff in jail. I've never been there. Neither has Therese. There — I think I heard the doorbell — my eyes pop back into my head with a scream — I won't open it — I'll climb out the window when they come. They won't get me! Never, never, never. Particularly now. I feel strong like a revolver. I'm a detective novel. Help me, dear God — I promise to cut "dear God" deep into my skin with a knife so it'll draw blood — if you let me get to Berlin safely.

It's quiet — it was just nerves. I'm biting my hand — it hurts so much that I stop being afraid.

So I was wearing my old rain coat — and Hubert — *Küppers Café* — no time to go home to change into the fox coat. I didn't know what to do. I so wanted to impress Hubert and shine for him. And we were taking our make-up off with grease — I had secretly taken margarine from home — and the porter comes in and calls in front of the door. I was to come to see the director. I got margarine in my eyes — God, did I feel awful. So it had finally happened. Leo — pajamas with roses — the girls were looking at each other, imagining wild passion. But I knew better. I only had the strength to secretly take the white feather off the *Wallenstein* hat — it's lying next to me now. I was hot with longing for Hubert, a man with a small indentation in his shoulder, where you can put your head and let the man be. You pay for that kind of longing. I knew it, but my feelings didn't feel like knowing it. Now the Trapper has my sentence, and I can only hope that she'll trip and fall when she dashes out of the tent. And so I packed up my little lump of margarine — why should that filthy theater get anything from me for free — and the eyeliners that were brand new.

And I went to the cloakroom of the dress circle to see my mother, who sometimes, sometimes understands my situation. But you can't understand another person when you're not surrounded by the same aura as they are, which causes them to do what they do. But my mother wasn't there — instead it was Frau Ellmann, the bitch, our neighbor. She was sitting there asleep, suffering, because she doesn't have to and for no good reason. And there was this coat — such sweet, soft fur. So fine and gray and shy, I felt like kissing it, that's how much I loved it. It spoke comfort to me, a guardian angel, protection from heaven. It was genuine squirrel. I quietly took off my rain coat and put on the fur coat, and started to feel guilty toward my abandoned rain thing, like a mother who doesn't want her child because it's ugly. But you should have seen me! And so I decided to present myself to Hubert like this, and put the coat back after the performance. But something inside me knew right away that I would never give it back again. And already I was too scared to come back to the theater later and having to talk to Leo and look at Frau Ellmann and hear her voice and all that.

And the fur coat was attached to my skin like a magnet and they loved each other, and you don't give up what you love, once you have it. But I was lying to myself all the way and truly believed that I would come back. The lining was crepe marocain, pure silk, hand embroidered. And so I went to *Küppers Café*. Hubert was sitting there with dark circles under the eyes, the size of *Continental* tires. He used to have skin like a baby — and it was all gone. And we said "du" to each other in such a formal way that it sounded like "Sie." But my mouth was open to his kisses, because he was sad. He admired me, which didn't make me feel good and didn't make me proud. I was surrounded by my coat, which had more feelings for me than Hubert.

And I knew right away that the true virgin had left him and that her father, the professor, hadn't given him a job, and that he was in trouble. And he says: "Doris, you're doing well, I can see. Therese told me about your career."

"Thank you," I said.

And Leo was waiting — because of the pajamas — it was late — the Ellmanns — I had been torn away from the world — and my furious father — everything was screwed up — and Hubert became a dead memory and wasn't really sitting there alive, in front of me — I tried to conjure up feelings for him, and it was like looking at his photograph when I'm drunk and wanted to believe that it was talking to me, and when I tried really hard I could sometimes make myself believe that it did.

And then I went with him. And I slept with a photograph. It was very cold. And he asked about my income and wanted help. I don't have anything. And I said Therese has some cold cuts, it's not as fancy as it looks, and I was tempted to tell him it was all over.

And I tried and said: "Hubert, you don't have anything, I don't have anything, that's enough — let's make something out of nothing together." And a disappointment came over him that made me sick to my stomach.

So I washed my face. It was a dark morning and I saw his face in bed, and it made me feel angry and disgusted. Sleeping with a stranger you don't care about makes a woman bad. You have to know what you're doing it for. Money or love.

So I left. It was five in the morning. The air was white and cold and wet like a sheet on the laundry line. Where was I to go? I had to wander around the park with the swans, who have small eyes and long necks that they use to dislike people. I can understand them but I don't like them either, despite the fact that they are alive and that you should take pity on them. Everyone had left me. I spent several cold hours and felt like I had been buried in a cemetery on a rainy fall day. But it wasn't raining or else I would have stayed under a roof, because of the fur coat.

I look so elegant in that fur. It's like an unusual man who makes me beautiful through his love for me. I'm sure it used to belong to a fat lady with a lot of money — unfairly. It smells from checks and Deutsche Bank. But my skin is stronger. It smells of me now and *Chypre* — which is me, since Käsemann gave me three bottles of it. The coat wants me and I want it. We have each other.

And so I went to see Therese. She also realized that I have to flee, because flight is an erotic word for her. She gave me her savings. Dear God, I swear to you, I will return it to her with diamonds and all the good fortune in the world.

2

LATE FALL AND THE BIG CITY

'm in Berlin. Since a few days ago. After an all-night
train ride and with 90 marks left. That's what I have to
live on until I come into some money. What I have
since experienced is just incredible. Berlin descended on
me like a comforter with a flaming floral design. The
Westside is very elegant with bright lights — like fabulous stones, really expensive and in an ornate setting. We
have enormous neon advertising around here. Sparkling
lights surround me. And then there's me and my fur coat.
And elegant men like white-slave traders, without exactly
trafficking in women at the moment, those no longer exist
— but they look like it, because they would be doing it if
there was money in it. A lot of shining black hair and deep-

set night eyes. Exciting. There are many women on the *Kurfürstendamm*. They simply walk. They have the same faces and a lot of moleskin fur — not exactly first class, in other words, but still chic — with arrogant legs and a great waft of perfume about them. There is a subway; it's like an illuminated coffin on skis — under the ground and musty, and one is squashed. That is what I ride on. It's interesting and it travels fast.

So I'm staying with Tilli Scherer in *Münzstrasse*, that's near *Alexanderplatz*. There are unemployed people here who don't even own a shirt, and so many of them. But we have two rooms and Tilli's hair is dyed golden and her husband is away, putting down tram tracks near Essen. And she films. But she's not getting any parts, and the agency is handling things unfairly. Tilli is soft and round like a down pillow and her eyes are like polished blue marbles. Sometimes she cries, because she likes to be comforted. So do I. Without her, I wouldn't have a roof over my head. I'm grateful to her and we're on the same wavelength and don't give each other any trouble. When I see her face when she's asleep, I have good thoughts about her. And that's what's important: how you react to someone while they're sleeping and not exerting any influence over you. There are buses too, very high ones like observation towers that are moving. Sometimes I go on them. At home, we had lots of streets too, but they were familiar with each other. Here, there are so many more streets that they can't possibly all know each other. It's a fabulous city.

Later on, I'll be going to a jockey bar with a white-slave trader type that I don't care about otherwise. But this way, I'll get introduced to the kind of environment that will open up some opportunities for me. Tilli also thinks that I should go. Right now I'm on *Tauentzien* at *Zunztz*, which is a café but without music, but cheap — and with lots of hectic people like swirling dust, so you can tell that something's going on in the world. I'm wearing my fur and am having an effect. Across the street is the Memorial Church that nobody can get into, because of the cars all around it, but it's an important monument, but Tilli says it's just holding up traffic.

Tonight I'm going to write everything down in order in my book, because there's so much material that's accumulated in me. So Therese helped me skip town that night. I was trembling all over and full of fear and expectation and joy, because everything would be new now and full of excitement and adventure. And she also went to my mother to fill her in and told her that I would pay back both her and Therese handsomely, if it all worked out. And I know that my mother can keep a secret, which is amazing because she's over 50, but hasn't forgotten what it used to be like for her. But they can't send me any clothes. That would be too dangerous — and so I've got nothing except for one shirt which I wash in the morning and then I stay in bed until it's dry. And I need shoes and many many other things. But it'll come. I also can't write to Therese because of the police who are undoubtedly looking for me — because I know the Ellmanns, how tenacious she is and how she enjoys making criminals out of people.

I don't care if she's in trouble because of me, because she was the one who cooked and ate Rosalie, which was our cat — a sweet creature with a silky purr and fur like white velvet clouds with ink spots. She used to lie on my feet at night and keep them warm — now I have to cry — I ordered a piece of cake for myself, Dutch kirsch, and now I can't eat it because I'm full of grief at the thought of Rosalie. But I took a doggy bag. And she had disappeared all of a sudden, without coming back, which she never did, because she was used to me. And I was standing at the window calling: "Rosalie" at night and into the gutters. I felt so sad that she was gone, not only because she kept me warm, not only my feet. And for something that's so small and so soft and helpless that you can pick it up with your two hands, you have to be full of love for that. And the next Sunday, I go upstairs to the Ellmanns to retrieve the celery slicer that she had borrowed from us, the bitch, because she won't ever buy anything that she can borrow from someone else. They were just sitting down for dinner — that unkempt Herr Ellmann, who looks like a missionary with those hypocritical eyes, sitting on an island unshaven and eating poor black people in order to convert them. His yellow teeth were sticking out of his mouth, that's how greedy he looked. And there was a platter on the table with fried meat on it — and I recognized the shape of Rosalie's body. Also, I could tell because of Frau Ellmann's behavior and her beady eyes. So I told her straight out, and she's lying in a way that I know; I'm telling the truth. And I break into tears in all my grief and smash the celery chopper into her face so her nose starts to bleed and her eye gets all black and blue. Which wasn't nearly enough, because Ellmann has work and they had enough to eat and didn't go hungry and so they didn't need Rosalie. My mother has been worse off many times, but we never would have dreamed of frying Rosalie, because she was a pet with human instincts — and that you shouldn't eat. And that's one reason I'm keeping the fur. Now I'm all worked up from those memories.

And I was on the road all night. One man gave me three oranges and he had an uncle who owned a leather factory in Bielefeld. He looked like it too. But since I had Berlin ahead of me — why should I have bothered with a guy who travels third class and has second-class airs, just because of leather uncles. That never makes a good impression. Plus he had oily hair, full of dust and grease. And smoker's fingers. And only an hour later, I knew of all the girls he'd had. Wild stuff, of course, and superwomen. And he broke their hearts, when he left them — and they'd throw themselves off church steeples, while taking poison and strangling themselves — so they would be dead for sure, and all that because of the leather guy. You know what men will tell you, if they're trying to convince you that they're not as miserable as they are. I, for one, don't say anything anymore, and pretend to believe it all. If you want to strike it lucky with men, you have to let them think you're stupid.

So I arrived at *Friedrichstrasse* Station, where there's an incredible hustle-bustle. And I found out that some great Frenchmen had arrived just before I did, and Berlin's masses were there to greet them. They're called Laval and Briand — and being a woman who frequently spends time waiting in restaurants, I've seen their picture in magazines. I was swept along *Friedrichstrasse* in a crowd of people, which was full of life and colorful and somehow it had a checkered feeling. There was so much excitement! So I immediately realized that this was an exception, because even the nerves of an enormous city like Berlin can't stand such incredible tension every day. But I was swooning and I continued to be swept along — the air was full of excitement. And some people pulled me along, and so we came to stand in front of an elegant hotel that is called Adlon — and everything was covered with people and cops that were pushing and shoving. And then the politicians arrived on the balcony like soft black spots. And everything turned into a scream and the masses swept me over the cops onto the sidewalk and they wanted those politicians to throw peace down to them from the balcony. And I was shouting with them, because so many voices pierced through my body that they came back out of my mouth. And I had this idiotic crying fit, because I was so moved. And so I immediately belonged to Berlin, being right in the middle of it — that pleased me enormously. And the politicians lowered their heads in a statesmanly fashion, and so, in a way, they were greeting me too.

And we were all shouting for peace — I thought to myself that that was good and you have to do it, because otherwise there's going to be a war — and Arthur Grönland once explained to me that the next war would be fought with stinky gas which makes you turn green and all puffed up. And I certainly don't want that. So I too was shouting to the politicians up there.

Then people were starting to disperse and I felt the strong urge to find out about politics and what those officials wanted and so on. Because I find newspapers boring and I don't really understand them. I needed someone who would explain things to me, and as part of the overall deflation of enthusiasm luck swept a man over to my side of the street. And there was still something of a bell jar of fraternization covering us and we decided to go to a café. He was pale and wearing a navy blue suit and was looking like New Year's Eve — as if he had just handed

out his last cent to the mailman and the chimneysweep.
But that was not the case. He was working for the city
and was married. I had coffee and three pieces of hazelnut torte — one with whipped cream, because I was
starving — and I was filled with a desire for political
knowledge. So I asked the navy-blue married man what
the politicians had come here for. And in turn he told me
that his wife was five years older than him. I asked why
people were shouting for peace, since we have peace or
at least no war. Him: "You have eyes like boysenberries."
I hope he means ripe ones. And so I was beginning to
become afraid of my own stupidity and asked carefully
why it was that those French politicians on that balcony
had moved us so much and if this means that everyone
agrees, when there's so much enthusiasm, and whether
there will never be another war. So the navy-blue married
man tells me that he's from Northern Germany and that's
why he's so introverted. But in my experience those who
tell you immediately: "You know, I'm such an introvert,"
are anything but, and you can rest assured that they're
going to tell you everything that's on their mind. And I
noticed that that bell jar of fraternization was starting to
lift off and float away. I made one more attempt, asking
him if Frenchmen and Jews were one and the same thing,
and why they were called a race and how come the na-
tionalists didn't like them because of their blood — and
whether it was risky to talk about that since this could be

the beginning of my political assassination. So he tells me that he gave his mother a carpet for Christmas and that he's terribly good-natured, and that he was telling his wife that it was unfair of her to criticize him for having bought himself a new silk umbrella instead of having the big easy chair reupholstered — which makes her too embarrassed to invite her lady friends over, one of whom is a professor — and that he had told his boss straight to his face that he didn't know anything — and that I had feelings in me, which is what he needed, and he was a lonely man and always had to tell the truth. And I know for a fact that those who "always have to tell the truth" are definitely lying. I lost interest in the navy-blue married man, since I was heavy-hearted and excited and didn't have the patience to flirt with a city official. So I said, "Just a minute," and secretly disappeared through the back door. And I was sad about not having gotten any political education. But I did have three pieces of hazelnut torte — which took care of my lunch, which couldn't be said about a lesson in politics.

I was negotiating with a traffic cop about how to get to *Friedenau*, which is where I needed to go, to Therese's old friend Margretchen Weissbach. I found her in a one-bedroom apartment where she was living with her unemployed husband. She was no Margretchen, but a real Margrete with a face that doesn't take life easily. And she was about to have her first baby. We said hello and immediately said "du," since we knew without exchanging a word that what had happened to one of us could just as easily have happened to the other. She's over thirty, but giving birth was easy nonetheless.

I had to call the midwife, since all her husband was capable of was smoking cigarettes at three pfennig apiece. I gave the midwife ten marks and told her to hurry up and that she should come to me for the rest of the money. And so I've been in Berlin for less than three hours and I already owe money to a midwife, which hopefully is not a bad omen. I sat next to Margrete while she was in labor. That's when you're ashamed not to be in pain yourself.

It was a girl. We called her Doris, because I was the only one there — besides the midwife of course, but her name was Eusebia. I spent one night on a mattress in case she needed someone after all. Next to me was the baby in a wooden box that she had filled with cushions and soft blankets with pink roses embroidered on them. On the other side of the baby slept her husband. His breath was hollow with happiness, because Margrete was okay — you could tell, even though he was all hard and grumpy. Margrete was asleep and he was saying things like: what were they going to do with a child, that already they didn't know what to do, and it would be better if the child had never been born. But during the night, I saw him bend over the wooden box, kissing the embroidered pink roses. I turned white with fear, because if he had known that I had seen him, he probably would have killed me. There are men like that. And Margrete thinks she can get another job at the office, now that it's all over.

In the morning, the baby was screaming like an alarm clock and we all woke up. The air felt like a round dumpling and you couldn't swallow it. The baby weighs eight pounds and is healthy. Margrete is breastfeeding, and she's well. Her husband was making coffee and milk. I made the beds. The man was black and angry. He was too ashamed to say nice things to Margrete, but we could tell that they were in him. Then he went out to look for work, but without any hope.

Margrete says that when he comes back, he will get mad at her and reproach her, and that's because he doesn't believe in what they call God. Because what a man like him really needs is a God whom he can blame and whom he can get mad at when things go wrong. This way he's got nobody who can be the target of his anger and hatred and that's why he blames his wife, but she minds — and the one who is called God doesn't mind — and that's why he should have a religion, or he should get political, because then he could also make a ruckus.

So I said goodbye to her, since I really couldn't stay there. Margrete gave me Tilli Scherer's address, a former colleague of hers who is also married, but her husband is frequently out of town. So I bought three diapers and I plan to have a green branch embroidered in the corner for good luck. And I will have them sent to the Weissbachs, since the child has been named after me.

And then I went to Tilli Scherer. She agreed to take me in. She too wants to become a star. And she won't take money from me. But every other morning, I will loan her my fur coat to wear at the film agency. I don't like to do that — not because I'm stingy, but because I don't like it to smell from anybody else. I've also tried film, but there's not much opportunity there.

Things are looking up. I have five undershirts made of Bemberg silk with hand-sewn seams, a handbag made of cowhide with some crocodile appliqué, a small gray felt hat, and a pair of shoes with lizard toes. But my red dress that I'm wearing day and night is starting to tear under the arms. But I've started to make contacts with a textile firm, which, however, isn't doing so well at the moment.

Overall, I can't complain. It all started on *Kurfürstendamm*. I was standing in front of a shoe store, where I saw such adorable shoes, when I had an idea. I went in with the assertiveness of a grand lady — helped by my fur coat — and tore off one of my heels and started to limp into the shop. And I handed my broken heel to the salesman.

And he calls me "Madam."

I say: "What a pity. I wanted to go dancing and I don't have time to go home and don't have enough money on me."

Needless to say, I left the store with lizard toes and that night I went to a cabaret with the salesman. I told him I was one of Reinhardt's new actresses. We both lied to each other tremendously and believed each other just to be nice. He's not stupid and he's a gentleman. He has a stiff knee and falls in love with women because he feels self-conscious about it.

At the Jockey Bar I met the Red Moon — his wife is on vacation, because times are bad and seaside resorts are cheaper in October than in July. He happened to be at the Jockey Bar by coincidence, as he's traditional and he's disgusted by the new times because of their lax morals and politics. He wants the Kaiser back and is writing novels and is well-known from the past. He also says that he has esprit. And his principle is: men can, women cannot. So I'm asking myself: How can men do it without women? What an idiot!

So he says to me: "Little woman" — and puffs himself up because he feels so superior to me. When he was 50, all the newspapers were in awe of him. And he had readers. He also has a degree and a cultural foundation. And he counts for something. He comes to the Jockey Bar to study. He's studying me too. He's written many novels for the German people, and now those little Jews are writing their decadent stuff. He's not going to play along with that.

So the Red Moon has written a novel, *Meadow in May*, that has been reissued hundreds of times, and he just keeps on writing and right now he's writing *The Blonde Officer*. And he invited me too. He has a beautiful apartment — full of books and so forth and a provocative chaise longue. I was drinking coffee and liqueur and eating a lot. The Red Moon was sweating and started to get heart palpitations, because we weren't drinking decaf. I didn't like it — the coffee or the Red Moon. But we had *Danziger Goldwasser,* which glitters in the small glass like a pond full of tiny gold pieces — they are swimming in it and you can't catch them, and it's highly uneducated to even try, and if you *do* try, then you scratch holes into your fingers and you still won't find anything — so what's the point of behaving in an uneducated way in the first place. But it's nice to know that you're drinking gold that tastes sweet and makes you drunk — it's like a violin and tango in a glass. I love you, my brown madonna . . . wouldn't it be wonderful to be with someone you like. Like, like, like. And he should have a voice as shiny as his hair — and his hands should be shaped so they could fit around my face and his mouth should be waiting for me. I wonder if there are men who can wait until you want to. There's always that moment when you want to — but they want to just a minute too soon, and that ruins everything.

Me — and my fur coat who is with me — my skin gets all tense with the desire that someone find me attractive in my fur, and I find him attractive as well. I'm in a café — violins are playing, sending a waft of weepy clouds into my head — something's crying in me — I want to bury my face in my hands to make it less sad. It has to work so hard, because I'm trying to become a star. And there are women all over the place, whose faces are also trying hard.

But it's a good thing that I'm unhappy, because if you're happy you don't get ahead. I learned that from Lorchen Grünlich, who married the accountant at Grobwind Brothers and is happy with him and her shabby tweed coat and one bedroom apartment and flower pots with cuttings and *Gugelhupf* on Sundays and stamped paper which is all the accountant allows her to use, just to sleep with him at night and have a ring.

And there is ermine and women with Parisian scents and cars and shops with nightgowns that cost more than 100 marks and theaters with velvet, and they sit in them — and everything bows down to them, and crowns come out of their mouths when they exhale. Salespeople fall all over themselves when they come into the store and still don't buy anything. And they smile when they mispronounce foreign words, if they do mispronounce them. And with their georgette adorned bosoms and their cleavage they sway in such a way that they don't need to know anything. Waiters let their napkins trail on the floor when they leave a restaurant. And they can leave expensive rump steaks and à la Meyers with asparagus on their plates without feeling bad and wishing that they could pack them up and take them home. And they hand the bathroom attendant thirty pfennigs without looking at her face to find out if her way makes you want to give her more than necessary. And they are their own entourage and turn themselves on like light bulbs. No one can get near them because of the rays they're sending out. When they sleep with a man, they breathe on pillows with genuine orchids, which are phenomenal flowers. And foreign diplomats admire them and they kiss their manicured feet in fur slippers and don't really concentrate, but no one cares. And so many chauffeurs with brass buttons take their cars to garages — it's an elegant world — and then you take the train to the Riviera in a bed to go on vacation and you speak French and you have pig leather suitcases with stickers on them, and the *Adlon* bows down to you — and rooms with a full bath, which are called a suite.

I want it, I want it so badly — and only if you're unhappy do you get ahead. That's why I'm glad that I'm unhappy.

Dear Mom, in my mind I'm sending my love to you and Therese. I miss you, but Tilli is good to me. But she's new to me and what's new can't replace the old for me — and the old is not the new. There's a void in me from your absence, and there are words and words piling up in my throat that I can't say to you — that instills so much love in me that I feel like I've been put through a meat grinder.

With you, I had familiar streets with pavement that said hello to my feet when I stepped on it. And there was the streetlight with the cracked glass and the scratched-up lamppost: Auguste is stupid. I scratched that in there eight years ago on my way home, and it's still there. And whenever I think of the streetlight, I'm thinking of you. I have a changed name and I'm always nervous and I'm not allowed to write to you because of the police — until grass grows over the whole thing. But I'm sending thoughts and love your way.

I went over to the Red Moon's house. So after the *Danziger Goldwasser* I got the tour of the apartment, which naturally always ends in the bedroom. There were two beds and one of them was covered with lots of newspaper because of the moths, and there was no atmosphere whatsoever. And the Red Moon turned on a hanging lamp and I saw five undershirts made from Bemberg silk that his wife at the spa had left behind, and the Red Moon was supposed to send them to her. So I immediately point out the stylish embroidery. I'll take one of them with me, I say, and am going to have it copied. So the Red Moon says, fine — and approaches me like a hurricane. The best thing to do in cases like that is to start talking about their profession, because that's as important to them as sex. So I stop his attack and ask him: "So what about that published meadow?" — and I put lots of interest in my eyes.

And he immediately goes for the bait and asks me if he should read to me. And I say yes with the enthusiasm of little kids if you ask them if they want to go to the zoo, and I sit down on the newspaper-covered bed. The Red Moon sits down on the other bed and starts to read — and goes on and on and on.

At first I was planning to listen — there was nothing but vineyards and girls dancing and braids coming loose, and then more vineyards without end. So I got bored — the braided maiden was feeding chickens, which she didn't have to do because she was financially secure — and the Red Moon made "putt putt putt" sounds in a high-pitched voice. So I think to myself, that's too much to ask, hours and hours of vineyards for nothing — and I take another shirt and stuff it into my dress. And every three pages he tells me that it's going to get more refined — and every five pages I take another shirt from the bedside table, until they're all gone. And then I get up and say: "I've heard the churchbells strike and I need peace and quiet to think about the vineyards." And I make off with a bust that would rival that of a first-class wet nurse.

And so I was taking care of obnoxious kids of a high-society onyx family, the incognito children of a former general's daughter. Tilli had arranged it — she used to watch the onyx kids. They live at the riverbend and they are knowingly insolent, like grownups. The husband has onyx and stocks and white hair that stands straight up, finding itself attractive. And he's tall and stately looking. The wife is young and lazy and doesn't know from anything.

If a young woman from money marries an old man because of money and nothing else and makes love to him for hours and has this pious look on her face, she's called a German mother and a decent woman. If a young woman without money sleeps with a man with no money because he has smooth skin and she likes him, she's a whore and a bitch.

Dear mother, you had a beautiful face, you have eyes that look like you desire something, you were poor as I am poor, you slept with men because you liked them or because you needed money — I do that too. Whenever anyone calls me names, they call you names as well — I hate everyone, I hate them, I hate them — to hell with the world, mother, to hell with it.

So there comes the White Onyx and says "Mademoiselle." And makes eyes at me and I was ready. The elegant noblewoman had gone to the theater and I was home with him, and he offered me an apartment and money — this was my opportunity to achieve glamour. It's easy with old men, when you're young — they pretend it's your fault as if you were the one who started it. And I wanted to, I really wanted to. He had the voice of a bowling ball that made my blood run cold, but I wanted to — he had this slimy look in his eyes, but I wanted to — I was thinking, I'll grit my teeth and think of fabulous ermine, and I'll be okay And I said yes.

And then came the hunk. He rang the doorbell and he came in and he was a guest, a former friend of the Onyx and not so young anymore — but gorgeous, just gorgeous. And we took one look at each other. And the three of us had a glass of wine. And all of a sudden it occurred to me that I was rich, because I could afford to do something stupid. Yes, yes, yes, I was so stupid. I made a face at the Onyx — and there were diamonds in my heart, because I was rich enough to do what I wanted.

I went with the hunk. He was tall and slender. And he had a dark face like a powerful fairy tale. My dreams were kissing me mad. The room was cold and dark, but the hunk was shining. I kissed him gratefully, because I didn't have to be ashamed to see him naked. I put gratitude into my hands, because I didn't have to lie ambiance into my pillow, when he took off his clothes — my skin was warm with gratitude, because there was nothing ugly about him that I would have to ignore, once the lights came on. Oh my God, I was such a grateful creature because he pleased me so much.

That says a lot, if somebody pleases you — love is so much more that I'm thinking, perhaps it doesn't exist at all.

But handsome one, why did you make such a stupid mistake? To tell the Onyx that I was with you last night?

So the Onyx says to me: "You are a whore, get away from my pure children." And the noblewoman breathes a sweet sigh: "I simply cannot believe it!" So I say: "It's not like your pure children were fathered by the Holy Spirit, but rather by an old Onyx the ordinary way."

And I left without having to be told, and in my heart were such diamond kisses of stupidity that I couldn't eat. And with my last paycheck, I bought myself a honey brown dress with smooth pleats, quiet and serious, like a woman who forgets to laugh when she's being kissed by someone she likes.

As soon as Tilli's husband returns, I'm going to have to leave, which scares the hell out of me. It's less because I won't have a roof over my head anymore than because I won't have anyone at all. And Berlin is fabulous but it's not homey, because it closes itself off. And that's also because people here have tremendous problems, and that's why they have little compassion with those who have fewer problems than they — but mine are plenty for me.

I told Rannowsky: "This is going too far. Don't even think of talking to me about that. Who do you think you are?" Because he's a word that I would be ashamed to put on paper and he lives in the apartment above us — he's a pimp. And this is really the kind of apartment complex where everybody knows everyone else's secrets that they would be better off knowing nothing about. He was a laborer and was supposed to be promoted to supervisor in his factory. And right at that moment, he lost his job and cut up the drive belts, because he was so mad. So they threw him in jail, but for real. And now he has four girls who do for him, well, the lowest thing you could be doing. Still that doesn't mean that he should beat them, which he does in a way that Tilli and I are afraid the ceiling will come down some night and the whole gang will fall right on top of us. And his hair stands straight up, and in my experience, that's a sure sign of brutality. And he's only 30. So last night he was sitting on the stairs, drunk of course, and I'm trying to get past him. He grabs my foot: "Holy God, now he's going to kill me!" "Let go of me, Herr Rannowsky, I beg you." And he starts to weep and says: "I'm done for, I have no one left, only my goldfish." So I say to him: "You should be ashamed of yourself. Why do you have to beat the lowliest of all girls who give you money?"

"It's my muscles," he says, "and I hate it that they give me money, because they are such pigs."

And I: "They have to work."

But of course that was all nonsense. And he spits on my left suede pump and says he finds women disgusting. But he has four goldfish; the greatest of all of them is called Lolo. They have eyes and they look at him when they expect food, and they're good and decent. But if you ask me, it's because that's all they're capable of.

I'm scared to turn into one of Rannowsky's women. Berlin makes me tired. We have no money, Tilli and I. We stay in bed, because we're so hungry. And I still owe Therese. It's hard for me to find work, because I have no papers and can't register with the police, because I'm living underground. And people treat you badly and they're cheap, if they notice that you're not doing well. I want to become a star. Today, we're going to the Resi — Franz invited me. He works at a garage.

Das ist die Liebe der Matrosen . . . and the telephone rings — rrrrr — at all the tables. They have real keys and you can dial. Berlin is so wonderful. I would like to be a Berliner and belong here. The Resi, which is behind *Blumenstrasse*, isn't a restaurant really. It's all colors and whirling lights, it's a beer belly that's all lit up, it's a tremendous piece of art. You can find that sort of thing only in Berlin. You have to picture everything in red and shimmery, more and more and more, and incredibly sophisticated. And there are luminescent grapes and large tureens on posts, but the lids are separate — and they glitter and there are fountains that spray a very fine mist. But the audience is not first class. They have a mail chute — you write letters and put them into a hole in the wall. Then there's a draft that whisks them toward their destination. I was completely in a trance because of all of this.

Franz from the garage ordered Italian salad and wine for me. And whenever he had to step out, my phone would ring. I love getting phone calls — once I'm a star, I'm going to have my very own telephone that rings and I'm going to go: "Hello" — with my chin pressed down on my chest and completely blasé like a top manager.

Das ist die Liebe der Matrosen . . . and that generously decorated ceiling is making a turn to the right, and the floor that I dance on is turning to the left — aye aye, Captain, aye aye . . . that kind of thing makes you drunk without a drop of alcohol.

Franz has limp hair and a bad back, because of his mother whom he supports and his three little brothers. He hardly ever goes out but when he does, he has to get drunk, because otherwise, he won't have the courage to be really happy and forget that he's spending money on himself. He's attached to his family. And I realized that as the night went on, and from then on the wine didn't taste so good to me anymore. I wanted to be with someone who can spend money at night without missing it in the morning.

Aye, aye, Captain, aye, aye Cap — good night, wonderful colorful colors.

My life is Berlin and I'm Berlin. And it's a mid-size town after all, where I'm from, and the Rhineland with industry.

And my father wasn't really my father, he just took me on when he married my mother. My mother had had a life, but was still a solid person and not stupid. And at first he didn't want me and he went to court because of child support, which all men who possibly qualified as my father blamed me for. And he lost the case. But it had to have been someone, after all. And they never beat me, but that was about the only positive thing that could be said about their parenting. And then school. My mother had made me a good dress from the curtain, because of the people next door — so they would be angry, not so I would be happy. And all it did for me was give me the constant fear that I would get my dress messed up, and the boys in my class called me smarty pants. And the girls from the high school across the street would look at me and say: "Look at that one with the funny dress!" And they would laugh at me. The dress was all sticking out around me and it was dark green with a pattern of animals with long tongues on it — and all the kids were laughing at me. And now I'm wearing a fur coat, and I'm in Berlin! And I would throw rocks at them and swear to myself that I would not be the kind that is laughed at, but that I would do the laughing.

And then I got an apprenticeship. Right now I'm passing through a sea of lights. And once I was sick. Parents feel love toward their kids when they're sick and could die from a fever. That's when they sacrifice themselves. But as soon as you're better, they forget about their fear. I couldn't get a job because I was too weak, and so I immediately turned into a burden. And that's the way it happens with everybody.

Everyone should come to Berlin. So beautiful. You can buy potato pancakes from an open shop window. It used to be the Ruhrbeins, my relatives, who would always eat potato pancakes — and there was Paul, my cousin, unemployed and wearing the suits of his older brother, who was making a living, but he couldn't find anything and was just sitting there. And he would rest his elbows on the kitchen table, and my aunt would say: "Paul, please, don't do this. You have to take good care of this suit. You didn't pay for it."

I guess they comforted him when he was desperate and crying, and they always really resented it when he was in a good mood.

I'm walking through *Friedrichstrasse* and I'm looking and I see shiny cars and people, and my heart is a heavy blossom.

And one day we were all at the Ruhrbeins — I just saw a wreath, that makes me happy — and we were sitting there, and Paul was really happy because everyone was in a good mood, and so he said: "Why don't we go get a bottle of wine, Mother?"

So she looks at him and in a hissing voice all angry she says: "As soon as you start to make money again, you can go ahead and offer your friends some wine."

We all turned red and the room went silent. And Paul left and that same night he took his own life, drowned himself. And the Ruhrbeins cried terribly and were united in their sorrow and saying: "He was the best of all of our kids, and how could he do this to us, when we've always been so good to him?"

That's the way it always goes with the children of poor people. I do love my mother and I miss her, yet I'm so glad I'm away from home and in Berlin, and I'm free and am going to become a star.

I'm walking at night and in the morning — it's a crowded city with lots of flowers and shops and lights and restaurants with doors and felt curtains behind them — I'm trying to guess what's inside, and sometimes I even go in to take a look and pretend I'm looking for somebody who isn't there, and then I leave. And sometimes I stay, if it's a very interesting place. I've even had asparagus salad in Berlin.

And last night, a man took me home in his car. Because he hadn't shaved, my face is completely prickly today, and I'm as red as a tomato and kind of sunburnt. That just goes to show you that you can never be too careful when it comes to men. But it's spring, and Berlin is like Easter and Christmas combined for me. Everything is full of shimmery business. I see men and I'm thinking to myself, there are so many of them. There's got to be someone for me, who's breathing Berlin. And he will have black hair and a bowtie of white silk.

I love Berlin, but my knees are trembling and I don't know what I'm going to eat tomorrow. But I don't care.

I'm sitting at *Josty's* at *Potsdamer Platz* and I'm surrounded by marble columns and an incredible vastness. Everyone is reading the paper and foreign ones with important headlines and they have a calmness to them as they sit there, as if they owned everything, because they're able to pay. Me too today.

I went to *Leipziger Platz* and *Potsdamer Platz*. You can hear the music from the movie theaters. It's on records, which is a way of preserving people's voices. And everything is a song.

Downstairs from us lives Herr Brenner, who can't see anymore — no shops or checkered lights or modern advertising or anything at all. Because he lost his eyesight in the war. And his wife is old and angry. She thinks everything should belong to her, because she makes all the money and is ironing day in and day out for people and making clothes — beats me who would buy something that unfashionable. And so she has earned her husband as he gets nothing and has no social security, because he's from the Alsace, but he fought for the Germans. And he's about 40 years old and is sitting around all day, sad and staring at the wall, which he can't see. And he has such beautiful lips. I visit him sometimes, when his wife is away, because she doesn't want me around. She wouldn't even want the dirt from her kitchen floor to stick to other people's feet. And so she won't have anyone in the kitchen that is hers, and it's her husband, too.

I can understand why men are unfaithful. When women own something completely, they sometimes have a way of being good that borders on meanness. And that kind of woman doesn't give you any room to breathe. Brenner is a fine man and has a lot of thoughts that he tells me about. And all his thoughts are in the kitchen, and when his wife is there she fills up the kitchen with her voice and cries because of him and complains that she has to work so hard. Then there's no more room for his thoughts in the kitchen.

And then he says to me: "Whenever she's crying, I have to think that she has long yellow teeth," and then he asks me: "Does she have long yellow teeth?"

I tell him, "No, she has little white teeth" — even though it's not true. But it must be awful to be thinking of those long yellow teeth all the time.

I collect images for him. I walk around the streets and the restaurants and among people and lanterns. And then I try to remember what I've seen and bring it to him.

Just now a bureaucratic type is approaching me with a handkerchief with green trim and a monocle.

So Brenner with his pale hands asks me: "What do you actually look like?"

And I'm sitting right in front of him on the kitchen table and even though I wiped it off with that stinky rag first, I can be sure to have a grease spot on my butt when I get up. But it's an old dress. I've put my feet on top of his knees, as he sits opposite me stroking my silky legs. He doesn't have any other pleasure in life.

The air is humming yellow. And so he asks me: "What do you look like?" That was really strange. I wanted to see myself from the outside, not like a man would usually describe me, which is always just half the truth anyway.

And I'm thinking: Doris has turned into an enormous man with great erudition and is looking at Doris and says to her like a medical doctor: "My dear child, you have a nice figure, perhaps a bit thin, but that's fashionable right now, and your eyes are a black-brown like those ancient silk pompons on my mother's pompadour. And I have something of an anemic paleness and I have red cheeks at night and when I'm excited. And my hair is black like a buffalo, well not entirely. But well, kind of. And frizzy because of my perm, which is already starting to relax a bit. And I have thin pale lips by nature. With sensual make-up. But I have very long lashes. And very smooth skin without freckles or wrinkles or dust. And everything else is very nice, I think."

But I was ashamed to talk about my stomach, which is first-class and white, and I do think that all girls find themselves attractive when they stand in front of a mirror naked. And when you're naked with a man, he's so crazy already that he thinks everything is beautiful and that way you never really get a true opinion on your body.

"I can't hear you walking," says Brenner. "How do you walk, do you move your hips?"

And I tell him: "No, I can't stand it when girls wiggle their behinds like a corkscrew when they walk. But sometimes, my feet are bouncing and I have a wonderfully exciting feeling in my knees." And then I couldn't go on talking, because I think "thighs" is such a terribly naughty word. But what else can you say when you talk about what's above your knees?

And over in the corner is a cockroach and everything is gray and without any elegance. It was disgusting. He didn't have the courage to kiss me. That gave me courage and love. I used to think you could help people only with money. Actually, you can't really help anyone, but you can give them pleasure — and that's nobody's business, not my dove-covered notebook's or mine or anybody's.

Brenner strung up a necklace of wooden beads for me. They are a beautiful red and green and are put together with a system. And he's blind! I'm not an idiot and I certainly have ambition, but I cried with joy because it's very rare that you still get a present afterward.

Tilli says: "Men are nothing but sensual and they only want one thing." But I say: "Tilli, sometimes women too are sensual and want only that one thing." And there's no difference. Because sometimes I only want to wake up with someone in the morning, all messed up from kissing and half dead and without any energy to think, but wonderfully tired and rested at the same time. But you don't have to give a hoot otherwise. And there's nothing wrong with it, because both have the same feeling and want the same thing from the other.

So I'm living in Berlin, first for myself and secondly for Brenner. And I'm sitting in the kitchen and the bed is behind a curtain. If it were up to me, I would hang the curtain — which is covered with stains — in front of the stove rather than the bed.

And then there's him with his thin lips and features like a child that has fallen and hurt himself and his hair is falling into his face, and he's wearing a Tyrolean jacket. And I'm in front of him on the table and sometimes I love his hands around my feet.

This has got to be the first time that a man's hands have known exactly when I don't like them to be moving. I'm telling you. There are only two types of men: those who have a thousand hands, and you don't know how on earth you're going to get them off you, and those with only two hands that you can deal with, simply by not wanting them to touch you.

And he put his hands around my feet as if they were Christmas candles — at home, we keep our Christmas tree candles for three years, because we only light them while singing *Silent Night, Holy Night*.

And there's a silence and a steamy humidity and the gray wall in front of the window. All that is falling right on top of us. I'm sitting there powdering my face because of his hands. And I'm fixing my lipstick. But he can't tell when I look beautiful. I offer him Berlin, which is resting in my lap.

And he asks me: "Dear voice of a folk song, where did you go today?"

"I was on *Kurfürstendamm*."

"What did you see?"

And I must have seen lots of colors there: "I saw — men standing at corners selling perfume, without a coat and a pert face and a gray cap on — and posters with naked and rosy girls on them and nobody looking at them — a restaurant with more chrome than an operating room — they even have oysters there — and famous photographers with photos in showcases displaying enormous people without any beauty. And sometimes with."

A cockroach is crawling around — is it always the same one? — and there's no air in the apartment — let's smoke a cigarette —

"What did you see?"

"I saw — a man with a sign around his neck, "I will accept any work" with "any" underlined three times in red — and a spiteful mouth, the corners of which were drawn increasingly down — and when a woman gave him ten pfennigs, they were yellow and he rolled them on the pavement in which they were reflected because of the cinemas and nightclubs."

"What else do you see, what else?"

"I see — swirling lights with lightbulbs right next to each other — women without veils with hair blown into their faces. That's the new hairstyle — it's called 'wind-blown' — and the corners of their mouths are like actresses before they take on a big role and black furs and fancy gowns underneath — and shiny eyes — and they are either a black drama or a blonde cinema. Cinemas are primarily blonde — I'm moving right along with them with my fur that is so gray and soft — and my feet are racing, my skin is turning pink, the air is chilly and the lights are hot — I'm looking, I'm looking — my eyes are expecting the impossible — I'm dying to eat something wonderful like a rumpsteak, brown and with white horse-radish and pommes frites. Those are elongated homefries — and sometimes I love food so much that I just want to grab it with my hands and bite into it, and not have to eat with forks and knives — "

"What else do you see, what else do you see?"

"I see myself — mirrored in windows and when I do, I like the way I look and then I look at men that look back at me — and black coats and dark blue and a lot of disdain in their faces — that's so important — and I see — there's the Memorial Church with turrets that look like oyster shells — I know how to eat oysters, very elegant — the sky is a pink gold when it's foggy out — it's pushing me toward it — but you can't get near it because of the cars — and in the middle of all this, there's a red carpet, because there was one of those dumb weddings this after-noon — the *Gloria Palast* is shimmering — it's a castle, a castle — but really it's a movie theater and a café and Berlin W — the church is surrounded by black iron chains — and across the street from it is the *Romanisches Café* with long-haired men! And one night, I passed an evening there with the intellectual elite, which means 'se-lection,' as every educated individuality knows from do-ing crossword puzzles. And we all form a circle. But really the *Romanisches Café* is unacceptable. And they all say: 'My God, that dive with those degenerate literary types. We should stop going there.' And then they all go there after all. It was very educational for me, and like learning a foreign language.

"And nobody has much money there, but they're alive and part of the elite and instead of having money they play chess, which is a checkered board with black and blonde squares. They have kings too. And ladies. And it takes a long time, which is the whole point of it. Of course, the waiters don't like it, because a cup of coffee only has a five-pfennig tip in it, which is very little for a chessy guest of seven hours. But it's the cheapest occupation for the elite, because they're not working and that's why they're keep-ing busy. And they are very literary, and the literary elite is incredibly busy with their coffee and chess and talking and all that intellect, so they won't let on to themselves that they're lazy. Some are from the theater too, and very colorful girls that are very self-assured, and a couple of older men with trembling bodies that have something to do with math. And most of them are desperate to get published. And they criticize everything.

"That gave me a lot of material to work through. So I made myself a list of foreign words and wrote next to them what they meant. In some cases, I had to find out on my own. Those words make quite an impression when you use them. We artists were hanging out together — sometimes a few guys with beer bellies came walking by. They just look at us and they don't belong. We look down on them. So I throw my head way back as they are talking and stare at the sky and don't listen. And all of a sudden I press my lips together very tight and then I loosen them and blow smoke through my nose and full of nonchalance I throw a single foreign word at them. Foreign words used all by themselves are a symbol, I'll have you know, and a symbol fits into any context. If you have enough self-confidence, nobody dares admit that they don't understand. With a symbol you can never go wrong. But after a while I got tired of them anyway."

"What else, what else?"

"And there's a traffic light that changes from green to red and yellow — huge eyes and cars wait in front of it — I walk down the *Tauentzien* — and shops with pink corsets also sell green sweaters — why? And ties and a striped bathrobe for a man in the window — I see it — there are brown shoes and a fast food restaurant with Wagnerian music and sandwiches aligned in the shape of a star — and there are delicacies in the kitchen that I'm ashamed to never have heard of. And at *Zuntz*, you can smell the coffee. It's small and brown and lies in large flat baskets that look like the South. It's all so wonderful — and there are wide tracks of rails and yellow trains. And people at the *KaDeWe*. It's so big and with clothes and gold and many elegant little dogs on leashes at the door, waiting for ladies shopping inside — and enormously square — and a little *Wittenberg* Temple that has a train running in its belly — with a large lit-up U in front of it.

"And a blonde man with a monocle invites me — he has teeth like a mouse and a disgustingly small mouth that's all shiny and makes the monocled man look naked. We're drinking wine in a highly respectable restaurant. He's in insurance and talking without end and loud without any inhibition and he's an idiot and talking about his mother, to whom he gave a carpet as a gift — and someone sold him a cigarette lighter that didn't work and then wouldn't repair it for him for free — and 3 mark 80 is a lot of money — he doesn't throw his money out the window, but he does have to have his three beers every night together with his friends. After that, he goes to see his mother — after the third beer, every night. There are some who don't do that — he can't stand to be ripped off, that really makes him mad, and then that thing with the cigarette lighter — and I should come visit him, and that he knows restaurants where you can get a lot to eat for very little money, and you get seconds on potatoes and vegetables — and his foot is coming dangerously close to me — he just can't get over that cigarette lighter — and he won't give anything to the broken man with the pink bandaids, because what would happen if you started to give to everybody. I was thinking that too. He has to get to know the poor person first, since he had a bad experience once when he gave his roll to a beggar, because he had a bad stomach from the roast the night before and had sued the cook, and there was a thick layer of butter on the roll — and when he comes downstairs, both sides of the roll are stuck to the door — since then, he's changed, also when it comes to Jews — and he shows me the chintzy cigarette lighter — and Gandhi wasn't his cup of tea either, and a real man doesn't drink goat milk all the time, that's decadent, but more than three beers is no good either, a glass of wine maybe but no schnapps, because that's how a friend of his became a bailiff. He was studying to become a lawyer, and then the schnapps, and no degree — and the cigarette lighter — and that's when I had enough of the clean-shaven insurance guy — "

And we were laughing, Brenner and I.

"What did you see, what — "

I unpack my eyes for him — what else did I see?

"I went further down *Ansbacher Strasse* — there's a

store that sells precious stones, one kind is called amethyst, which practically already sounds purple, doesn't it?"

"And what else, what else?" — you can hardly breathe in that kitchen, and God knows when his wife is coming back — "Is this what Berlin smells like?" he asks as I hold my powder puff up to his nose — "What else — what else?"

"On *Nürnberger Strasse* there's a restaurant with gathered curtains that only Russians go to — it has wallpaper that reminds you of frozen cherries with sunny flowers — very funny — and an old Russian Moscow as a picture and a tiny madonna in the corner. And small lamps, a little bit white and a little bit red, if you're tall you'll hit your head on the ceiling. I'm all by myself, learning the menu by heart because of the Russian words that go with the sound of the music. I drink something yellow called Narsan — they also have *Schachly* from the Caucasus and *Watrushki* or something like that with cheese. The girls are wearing little white aprons and they're pretty, like dolls with big eyes and Russian language — and with their elegant faces they can prove to anyone that they are the wives of generals. The men have small black toothbrush-like mustaches — the band is singing — it's a language that sounds like soft mayonnaise, so sweet. The ceiling is a marbled grayish green — I see, I see — those general waitresses are so pretty — the music has bald spots and violins — a woman wearing a yellow blouse is laughing in Russian — men are happy without women and drunk without wishes and are hugging each other because they're full of booze and love for everything — at the back wall there's a mirror, it makes you look pale, but pretty — they have deep, dark eyes that are brown like the violin — you can be so wrong about these things — a handsome man just kissed a woman fat as a tadpole — old men are kissing each other — the music goes one-two, one-two — there are lamps hanging from the ceiling that look like Paul's starfish collection stuck together — the music is covered with flowers like a chiffon dress which tears very easily — let me tell you, Herr Brenner, a woman should never wear artificial silk when she's with a man. It wrinkles too quickly, and what are you going to look like after seven real kisses? Only pure silk, I say — and music — "

"What else, what else — "

Pure silk — Hubert once gave me a passionate kiss on the eyes, or on the eyelids rather — and so I had a tiny red spot on each eye — and was terrified at home — I couldn't move my eyelids during lunch on Sunday — and I stared in front of me until I had tears in my eyes. "Why are you making eyes like a crazy woman?" asked my father, but I keep staring — and that's just the way I have to stare now, because I have to see so much.

"Light gray suits really make dark men look like demons. Red ties make them look funny — my eyes are all worn out — you, you, you — "

"What else, what else?"

"The women in Berlin are beautiful and well groomed and in debt.

"I'm dancing, yes, I'm dancing — I'm choking — there's a Russian inside of me — he's an emigrant — the way he's talking — his words stumble rough and softly like the wheel of a Mercedes rolling over cobblestone pavement — he has no hair, his eyes are young and hard. And he's slender. And the woman with her white face and her strawberry mouth is pulling her badger over her left shoulder in a way — and with her left hand she says to my Russian: 'You, monkey, are none of my business really, but I wanted to — I like the way you look!' — and she says it with elegant disdain. I'm thinking, you bitch! 'Interesting woman,' says the Russian. 'But crooked legs,' I say in a cold voice. 'How do you know?' 'Because of the timid way she holds on to her glass and wants to go to the bathroom, but doesn't dare to go.' Believe me, whenever a woman wants to take a guy away from me, I have an elegant way of badmouthing her, I don't really know how I do it, but somehow I become intelligent all of a sudden. And we kiss while we're dancing — in a bar — the cocktails are colorful — the color of a bleached brimstone butterfly — you get a headache after — "

The wooden armoire is creaking, and Brenner puts his head on my legs: "I know you, I don't have to see you."

I think about what he said even though I don't really have time to think about words — I have a lot of love that

I'm willing to share, but you have to give me enough time so I want to. Tilli is crying because her husband has been unfaithful — because it could have been just any woman for him. All I say to Tilli is: "You should know that it could have been any other woman instead of you too. It's no different. And love is when you're drunk together and you want to do it and everything else is nonsense."

"Love is more than that," says Brenner.

"Love is a lot of different things," I say.

"Love is not business," he says.

"Pretty girls are business," I say, "and that has nothing to do with love. I know, I know — love so well — but I don't want to know it, I don't want to."

"But I have a longing in me," says Brenner. Why is it that his eyes are turning even more dead than before? I'm going to kiss him.

I love you, my brown madonna — Virgin Mary, please pray for us — those dead eyes are telling me: "Doris, the time has come. The day after tomorrow I'm going to go into a nursing home." The wife can't handle it any more and wants it this way. But now she's sorry, because this is the end of her majestic rule since she has no more subjects. No one can be emperor all by himself.

All three of us are sitting in the kitchen. He's propped up on the chair, the wife is near the stove, and I'm in front of the bed — we're all standing there — "Frau Brenner, your husband wants to spend one evening just walking around the streets — I'm going to lead him — because he's going to the home, and there he's not going to see anything anymore," I say. He doesn't say a word, but earlier he was begging me. I have a bouquet of violets pinned to my lapel — it was given to me by a suitor yesterday — and it's breathing all blue in the kitchen. She's standing there, his wife — long and thin and with greedy teeth: "I'm going with him."

Her voice knocks out my violets. "He's going with me. I'm his wife."

"I'm going to go with him. I can show him a lot."

And he's not saying a word. The battle was going on above his head. All men are cowards. Then his wife starts to scream about all that she's done for him.

What use is it? He can't see us — but she smells old and I smell young. I don't love him, but I'm fighting for our evening because he wants it, I can feel it in my knees. Perhaps because it's the greatest gift for a woman to be allowed to be good to a man. And nothing else. And so I thank him for allowing me to be good to him, because usually they only love the nasty ones. And it's much more exhausting to be nasty. That kitchen voice is killing my violets, they are dying right into my skin. And here I'm fighting for his wishes, because he's tired. "My child." My voice is trembling: "Dear Frau, whatever belongs to you — just for one evening — one night off — we'll come back, I beg you."

"What nonsense to be begging! Her kind knows only to scream every cent she's earned through her yellow teeth. But I know what I want — my child, I'm not afraid — I still have some money. We can go anywhere we want."

"It's your choice," screams the Yellow Teeth. Poor men, they always have to choose — Hindenburg — women — communists — women. "Listen Frau, just one evening and only for three hours — there'll be enough hours left for you — so many." Her hands with their rusty skin are dangling in front of me. "Yes," she says.

So let's go — we leave — crisscrossing Berlin — we take taxis — his skin smells like black and white birch trees, that's how happy he is — because those don't smell — you can only see them, but he can't — that's why he smells like them.

"It's hard carrying a dead thing around with you," he says. True. My uncle once had to carry a dead body up from the river at night and he told me: "Dead bodies are heavy." Is everything a dead body? Let's get off and keep walking — with music in the background — and he was young and drowned in a kayak and with a white sweater. And he had a girl. And the moon was shining, the sun had borrowed it — let's move on.

We drink vodka in a Russian restaurant. They have schnapps here that tastes like a meadow — "and you know, the wallpaper, it's covered with flowers that are laughing their heads off" — I love you because I'm good to you.

And we keep going — there's a hard wind blowing and voices and streets — "Can you smell it if it's getting dark?" Something inside me dissolves in so much calmness — I'm holding his hand and he trusts me, when I guide him — I must not become this way. How am I ever going to get anywhere? Let's eat something.

We enter a restaurant on *Wittenbergplatz*. We're sitting by the window. He has to talk to me, or else I won't know that he's having a good time, because his eyes are mute and his mouth is bitter and all he's got left is his voice and a light. And through the slit in the dark forest green curtains, one can see the shimmer of red neon lights from afar. "Are you happy?" Sure I am. Beer is good when you're thirsty. "Does it taste blonde?"

Let's move on — I'm afraid that he's no longer happy, but there's a feeling of trust emanating from his arm. I'm his salvation at every intersection.

He's sucking in the air and asks me: "Are there any stars?"

I look for them.

"Yes, there are stars," I lie and I give them to him — there are no stars — but there must be some behind the clouds and they must be shining inside-out tonight. I love stars, but I hardly ever notice them. I guess when you're blind, you realize how much you forgot to see.

And then we go to a café — I give my heart to you, only to you — the violinist has a way of singing! We have something sweet that tastes pink — be happy — I want to, want to so badly. That let me get drunk.

"Doris — a forest," he says.

A forest? — but we're in Berlin. I'm not looking at anybody — I'm living only for you — that guy over there — live your own life, something from Sunday school which I used to skip and would go dancing instead — what do I care about God, while I'm still wondering where babies really come from — but you find out soon enough.

If only he would talk! We need to move on — occasionally there's half a star coming out but it can't compete with the neon lights and all that buzz around us. Sometimes I close my eyes for a moment when we get to a bus stop — strange how all those sounds enter you — it's getting quieter and quieter — let's go to the *Vaterland*. They've got to still be awake there. And we get on the bus and the bus skips across the pavement with us, even though it's so big and fat — oops — and it's so crowded and all the people are breathing into each oth-er's faces — and the upholstery exudes a strange smell. Berlin. It's Berlin I'm showing him.

The *Vaterland* has spectacularly elegant staircases like a castle with countesses in stride, and landscapes and foreign countries and Turkish and Vienna and summer homes of grapevine and that incredible Rhine valley with natural scenarios that produce thunder. We are sitting there and it's getting so hot that the ceiling is coming down

— the wine makes us heavy — "Isn't it beautiful here and wonderful?" It is beautiful and wonderful. What other city has this much to offer, rooms and rooms bordering on each other, forming a palatial suite? All the people are in a hurry — and sometimes they look pale under those lights, then the girls' dresses look like they're not paid off yet and the men can't really afford the wine — is nobody really happy? Now it's all getting dark. Where is my shiny Berlin? If only he weren't getting quieter by the minute.

Let's go. In the *Westend*, I know something wonderful — it's expensive — but I think I can still swing it. It's an elegant restaurant — I once went there with the intellectual elite — they have wine directly from Italy and people get wonderfully drunk and there are incredibly interesting women there and elegant people and everything is mysterious with low ceilings — and nobody has to feel ashamed for being different from the way they are during the day.

And I ask him: "Are you tired?"

"No, I'm not tired. I really want to thank you — do you think the home is going to have a garden?"

"Yes," I tell him. "There's going to be a garden."

All I want to do is cry. Let's go — everything looks different all of a sudden — in front of the *Vaterland*, someone is beating a poor girl — she's screaming — and a police officer arrives — a lot of people are standing around, not knowing where to go, and there's no glamour and nobody there — only dead tombstones — and if someone looks at you it's because he wants something from you — but why doesn't he want anything good? His leg movements are heavy and I can feel the pressure coming from him and now his heaviness is in me as well.

We're at the Italian place — they must not notice that he can't see. That would make them angry, because it disrupts the happy atmosphere. "It's nice here, isn't it?" Mosaic lanterns and quiet corners, but not the sleazy kind, much more elegant and in a deep red — the music is singing and there's an interesting buffet with oranges that look like leftover suns.

A St. Pauli girl, a girl from the *Reeperbahn*. "Oh my God! That's so zippy!" That's what Therese would say, because that's what her man used to say all the time — and that's the only sentence of his that she can remember. I'm going to start crying any minute now — and I'm telling jokes — my voice flickers like a fire that's about to die. He forces himself to laugh and says: "It's wonderful." But I don't believe him.

So he's not in love with me. That would salvage everything — but this way we're caught in this cold circle that only our heads can meet in and nothing else — and sometimes I have a feeling as if he were flying away from me on a heap of white cold snow — and then I'm freezing to death with loneliness — he's got to help me for a change — and when he's at the home and I don't see him anymore, he should have three good thoughts for me every day — that would really make a difference to me. I would find that very comforting — but maybe that's already too much to ask.

It's possible that I did love him a little bit — it's just that I don't want to and I'm fighting it because of my career and because it would only be trouble. But what can you do. You always notice too late that you're getting that stupid pain deep down in your stomach — he really could take my hand now.

"The city isn't good and the city isn't happy and the city is sick," he says — "but you are good and I thank you for that."

I don't want him to thank me. I just want him to like my Berlin. And now everything looks so different to me — I'm drunk and I'm dreaming with my eyes open — a St. Pauli girl, a girl from the *Reeperbahn* . . . and the band would much rather go home — a *Reeperbahn* girl really is much too sad a creature that she should constantly be cheering. And sometimes somebody is laughing — and that laugh is stuffing all of yesterday's and today's anger back into the mouth that it's oozing from. And I close my eyes — there's all that talk coming from so many mouths. They're flowing into each other like a river full of dead bodies. It's their funny words that have already been drowned in booze before they've had a chance to arrive at the next person's ear — and my uncle once carried one, with a white sweater and the moon was shining — why did we have to think of him earlier?

It was in St. Pauli near Altona that I was abandoned ... I love those songs — and at the table next to us, two men and a lady are introducing each other and are looking each other up and down with a friendly mistrust in their eyes and at first they want to believe only the bad things.

I'm talking to him and I finally want to find a word that makes me be with him — God, I can't stand it any more — let's go — What's wrong with me? — I want to kill that feeling inside of me. You have to be drunk to sleep with men, to have a lot of money — that's what you have to want and never think of anything else. How else are you going to stand it — What's wrong with this world?

And outside there're still no stars in the sky. We're leaving — I think the Memorial Church is telling a lie, saying it's a church — because if it were one, you should be able to go there and stay there right now. Where can I find love and something that doesn't fall apart right away? I'm so drunk, but I have to watch him — such a strange arm — back to his wife — back to the kitchen.

"The air is good now. It's lonely," he says — at *Kurfürstendamm* it's getting full again. At the corner, there are the voices of four young men. They have a musical instrument and the four of them are singing with a lot of hope in their voices: that's youth — that's love ... and we understand, and we listen, because a movement of his arm signals me to stop — and then they collect money and they're boys with happy faces, because they're not going to let themselves be broken and they're not afraid and they're walking with a secure step. And then they sing again, and everything in their voices is young — but I'm not old yet either, am I?

"That's beautiful," he says and he's breathing the voices and the air and the half stars — and then he searches his pockets for those pennies he saved up for tobacco at the home — and he gives them to the boys and says: "That was beautiful, four young voices that are holding together. Full of force, full of life, outside in the fresh air — that was beautiful."

But we didn't have to go all that way and all over the city for that. And all of a sudden, he tries to walk by himself — how can I let him! — but I'm very tired now.

Rannowsky from our building, who is a word that I'm ashamed to put on paper, has been arrested! Because he almost killed one of his women and she reported him. And now she keeps passing us on the stairs and her name is Hulla and she has a wide sagging face and hair that's been dyed yellow. Only blondes can look really mean, and it's hard to believe how a man could. . . . And she wears cheap, tight-fitting wool jumpers that emphasize her body shape in a vulgar way. So she stops me on the staircase and starts talking to me and I was beginning to feel creepy, because she comes from a terrible underworld that's completely foreign to me. That's how low you can sink. I was nice to her, because I was afraid of her and because nobody else is. I was a star compared to her.

The funny thing is that for every star there's one that shines even brighter. And she was trembling and begging me for money so she can feed the goldfish, because she's not able to make much money right now, that's how badly he's beaten her up.

And now he's in jail. And he's threatening her in his letters to her, telling her to take care of his goldfish, Lolo in particular: "Take care of my beloved babies, woman. Or else I'm going to break every bone in your body once I get out of here."

So we went upstairs to look at the fish and they were swimming back and forth and Lolo looked fat and lazy. "I just hope he's not sick," Hulla screamed in a high-pitched voice. And she looked terrifying with her face full of bandaids.

Tilli's Albert is back from Essen. "But you can stay," she tells me.

Sometimes he touches my arm in a way that ends my loneliness. But he's Tilli's!

I've made it. I am — Oh God! — mother, I've gone on a shopping spree. A little fur jacket and a hat and the finest saveloy — Is it a dream? I'm powerful. I'm bursting with excitement.

"Would you please air out my kimono," I tell my lady-in-waiting who always arrives in the disguise of a cleaning woman.

And he's calling me saying: "Dollface, fix yourself up. We're going to the *Scala* tonight."

And I'm living in a suite on *Kurfürstendamm*. Sometimes I spend three hours in the tub, bathing in scented bath salts.

He's like a jolly pink rubber ball. I met him in a café on *Unter den Linden*, where they play first-class music. I looked at him, he looked at me. I reminded him of a girl he had been in love with in high school — this has got to be three-hundred years ago, that's how old he is, but that's exactly what's so comforting to me.

I'm walking on carpets. My foot is sinking in as I'm turning on the radio: love, love is a heavenly force. And I'm so-o-o beautiful. And I almost have to cry, because now I don't know where to go with all that beauty — for whom am I beautiful? For whom?

He has a company that's struggling, and such comforting eyes.

"Alexander," I say, "Alexander, apple of my eye, king of hearts, my round little Gouda, I'm so-o-o happy!"

"Do you love me, just a teensy-weensy bit, my dove, or is it just my money?" he asks full of fear — and that moves me so much that I actually start to have some feelings for him.

For hours on end, Alexander tells me about his childhood and I'm listening, because he gave me the money to pay back Therese plus a portable gramophone and eighteen records by Richard Tauber, and one with my voice on it. I recorded it at *Tietz*, and I said: "Therese, I love you. Don't forget me. I might become a star in the movies, because Alexander thinks I have lots of talent. I'm riding around in a Mercedes and even the nails on my feet are polished, and I'm educating myself, and sometime I say 'C'est ça lala.' And I'm a lady. My shirts are made of embroidered *crêpe lavable* from Paris. I have a bra that cost 11 marks, and a pair of shoes made from genuine emu leather. I wish you could see me! 'Madam, where would you like me to take you?' asks Alexander's chauffeur. Good-bye Therese."

Once my mother wanted to have a canary. Therefore I had nine canaries transferred to her together with crystal flasks and lingerie and the like. I did the same for Therese. It's because I'm kind of homesick — and I'm so elegant, I could address myself as lady. I pick up the phone from my bed with its silk cover and dial a number and say: "Alexi, my ruby-red morning sun, why don't you bring me a pound of *Godiva*!"

"Aye, aye, dollface," he says, and I stay in bed resting in my lace nightgown or negligée. Sometimes I feel just the slightest bit bored. I gave Tilli a kayak.

Alex says: "Come on, dollface, let's have some champagne. My little Mickey Mouse, you're like a drop of dew."

He's a gentleman, even though he's short and fat. All his friends — all of them big industrialists — say to him: "Old curmudgeon, where did you find that beautiful woman?" and they kiss my hand.

Alexi seems nervous, and I say to him: "Child, you have to relax. Let's go to a spa."

"It's okay, it's okay, these are hard times," he says, and is talking all night long — that's how nervous he is.

"Why don't you consult a doctor, dear," I suggest, but he won't listen to me.

The apartment is so elegant, the chauffeur is so elegant, everything is fabulous. I stroll through the apartment. And there's dark red wallpaper, so incredibly elegant, and oak furniture and walnut. There are beasts on it with eyes that glow and you can turn them on electrically, and they start to eat smoke. And easy chairs with ashtrays attached to them like wrist watches — that's the kind of apartment it is.

And then I do something phenomenal. Clad in my negligée that surrounds my feet with its silky touch, I move forward, slowly lifting my lace-covered arms — and on my feet I have pink slippers with fur — and then I lift my arms as if I were on stage and I push open the big sliding doors and then I am on stage. In my opinion, sliding doors are the epitome of elegance. And so I close them again and then I go back and open them again — I'm a stage at least ten times every morning.

What a life! What a life!

I see a purse made of genuine crocodile — and I've already bought it.

I'm overwhelmed with myself.

All of a sudden, I can relate to Rannowsky's women and that Hulla with the bandaids on her face. What's the use of having all that money just for yourself? And when all you get are men that aren't any — just automatons, and you want to get something back from them — just get something and you throw yourself into it — eventually you want one who isn't just an automaton, whom you give something to. I've gone back to reading a lot of novels.

I bathe a lot.

As soon as the Gouda's wife comes back from her trip, I'm going to have to leave the apartment. What's a society? Am I society now? I have white silken gloves by Pinet at 40 marks and I can say *olala — c'est ça* in a way that makes everyone think I speak perfect French.

So he tells me: "Dollface, be true to me. You're going to have to be by yourself tonight." Tilli wasn't home. I went to a couple of bars. My fur. I tried to be tired, but I couldn't. Dear Mom, yesterday was Sunday, and you probably made red cabbage as usual. Did the house stink from vinegar again? But my mother uses only the best vinegar.

My head felt like an empty swirling hole. I created a dream for myself and rode up and down the streets of Berlin for hours on end, all by myself. I was a movie and a weekly newsreel all by myself.

And I did that because usually I get to take taxis only with men who want to smooch — and I would be with those whom I found disgusting, and then I needed all my energy to distract myself — or with those whom I liked, but then it was a sofa on wheels with wine and not a taxi. Just for once, I wanted a real taxi. And I occasionally had taken a cab by myself, if a man gave me the money to take a taxi home — but then I would sit on the edge of my seat and stare at the meter the whole trip. But today, I rode around in a taxi like rich people, leaning back in my seat and looking out the window — lots of cigar stores on the corners — and movie theaters — *The Congress Dances* — Lilian Harvey is blonde — bakeries — and lit-up street numbers on houses and some without — and tracks — yellow trams gliding past me and the people inside could tell that I was a star — I'm leaning way back in my cushions and I don't watch how the fare is adding up — I won't allow my ears to hear the click — blue lights, red lights, millions of lights — shop windows — dresses, but no models — sometimes other cars go faster — bedding stores

— a green bed that isn't really a bed, but more modern. It's flipping around itself, feathers whirling around in a large glass — people on foot — the modern bed turning.

I would so much love to be happy.

Thank God I was able to salvage the crocodile purse plus the white silk shoes plus a suitcase with at least some of my things, besides the fur. When his wife returned un-expectedly in the morning, I was still in bed. Later I told my lady-in-waiting that the opened bottle of cologne I had left behind was for her. I went to the post office to call the Gouda at the office. He's been arrested. Why? I'm sure it's because of money. Nowadays, the finest people end up in jail.

I went to Tilli and gave her the white silk shoes. She doesn't appreciate them enough, but she still would have taken me in even without them. That's why I gave them to her in the first place! And now what? Tilli's hard Albert is on the dole. Tilli cleans at Ronnebaum's.

I had to sell the crocodile purse way below cost.

Always the same. Always the same.

I run into the bandaid lady on the stairs. I have this desire in my gut to be liked by everybody. That always happens when nobody likes you.

Sometimes Albert takes my arm. Tilli loves him. She has to leave in the morning. Her eyes don't love me any more. Men are all the same. The hard guy is bored. Tilli is gone. I'm there. And new, so to speak. Sometimes my head wants to rest on his arm. That's why I get up really early and leave the house with Tilli and then I go for a walk.

It's almost Christmas.

They're always fighting. "No," Tilli tells me, "don't iron Albert's shirts." And then we're both all tears and kisses.

But I just talked to her. Dead. But she was nice. Hulla is dead. At the hand of Rannowsky. He got out of prison this morning. The main goldfish Lolo died because Hulla had retained a scar on her mouth from Rannowsky's beating, and it will never go away — that's what the doctor said. So she goes to the fish tank and takes out Lolo and puts him on the floor. She comes downstairs calling for me. So we both go up together. I say, "But Miss Hulla!"

That Lolo is lying on a piece of newspaper. She throws herself on the ground and screams: "Put him back in the water, bring him back to life, put him back in the water!"

I put him back in the water. His belly is up.

She says: "I didn't want that."

She's shaking her head — we never want that sort of thing. There's something there that makes sure that what we lied about wanting, but didn't really want, happens. We cried for that creature. We smoked a cigarette and then we cried some more.

"I fed him," says Hulla, "and last night a guy asked me, what's that on your face, are you sick? I fed him. So he asks, are you sick? I was asking for three marks, I needed new stockings — "

She shows me the runs in her stockings. And then she says: "We had agreed on 3 marks, and then he gives me 2.50 — and all I wanted was 3 marks — and three years ago, one man gave me 3.40 — it's unfair!" I agreed. "And then I go to the doctor: 'You'll never get rid of that,' now my face looks like I'm sick and I only get 2.50 — so I hated him, and since you can't get to the ones you hate, you ruin those you love, because you can get to them." And it's Rannowsky she hates — it's him.

And the fish continued to swim belly up. Three others hit him with their snouts. The dead fish's tummy was pale. And that overweight Hulla was kneeling on the floor praying. And she's terrified — "take care of my beloved fish, woman . . ." He's so brutal. And I say to her: "Hulla, I'll get us some cognac!" — after all, she was completely shaken up.

And Tilli wasn't there. So I say: "Albert, give me the bottle, please!" He's drunk and he grabs me. I say: "No — Albert, please, the goldfish!"

Why is it that God gave him this aura that I like — and I was so excited anyway. His eyes. Only for a moment. All that running on the staircase. Tilli — Hulla! And as I come upstairs, there's lots of people there. And Rannowsky. And

Hulla jumps out of the window, the moment he enters the room.

Sometimes there are mirrors that make me look like an old woman. That's the way it's going to be thirty years from now.

"But I'm not telling you to leave. I'm not telling you. Why don't you stay," said Tilli. So I left. Since I'm a thorn in her side and she's been so decent to me. I took a furnished room for a few days — as long as I can afford it.

The landlady's a bitch and the hallway is a pigsty and there's no light in the toilet, which is also the broom closet. To call this a furnished room! That's some way of being alone. But I don't care anymore. I'm putting all my eggs into one basket now. There are so many men, why shouldn't there be one for me for a change? I'm so sick of it all. Whenever they have money, they have stupid wives and get themselves arrested, is that fair? There's got to be something else in this world.

I tell old Reff about my landlady. "Frau Briekow," I say, "what do you mean, where are my handkerchiefs with the embroidered M on them?"

I stole them myself and don't have to have them stolen again by this stinky lump of horsemeat of a landlady. I can feel new energy in me. I just can't register. For my part, I have to say that I haven't had much fun with the police so far. I have to begin to consider all my options.

It's freezing in here. That crazy Albert! All trouble comes from those dumb jerks. On the other hand, you do need them. It's disgusting. Well, I could still try film. Then I can sit in the film café from morning till night, all year round. Some day they will discover me as a starved corpse to use as an extra. Dirty pigs.

Five pfennigs extra for a tiny pot of hot water, that Briekow is asking. Very soon she's going to position herself in the bathroom and take a penny each time. I could try bartending. The other night I was at a bar with the caterpillar. He latched on to me at the *Café des Westens* — plaid suit with a dotted tie, on his head more oil than hair and two cherry brandys and me with my genuine emu leather shoes for 40 marks! Girls were sitting on their barstools like plucked chickens on a ledge, looking as if they would have to go to a spa first before they would ever be able to lay another egg. And in front of them guys — like sensual rabbits sitting up on their hind legs groveling. And the way they talk! You really have to have been there. For a tip of three cents they talk for eight hours in front of a glass of eggnog — all lies of course. Then they tease you — and you have to listen to their jokes, too! If I were a bartender, I wouldn't laugh unless they gave me one mark. I would have the proper outfits. But unfortunately, I have no elegant evening gown. I'm going to the post office now to call Lippi Wiesel, who loved me back then. He's one of the intellectual elite but not that poor, because he's got a steady job at the news-paper and he's right where things are happening.

So I call Lippi Wiesel, who looks like one too, by the way. And I had a plan, because I had the reputation of being elegant in that group.

And so I say in a calm voice: "Hi, Lippi — how's it going — well — tell me, do you know Sweden?"

And he says "Yes."

Me: "That's where I had wanted to go at first. Do you know Greece?"

And he says "Yes."

Me: "I had considered going there too."

So I'm thinking what other countries are there where that son of a bitch might not have been, because I had my plan and had to impress him. So I ask: "Do you know Bulgaria?"

And he says "No."

And I'm thinking: Thank God! — and now I start my story: "So I was in Bulgaria. My father has a secret con-nection with the government there — yes, I just got back a little while ago — no, my father is still there. I had something going with the secretary of acquisitions — very uncomfortable — you know, if you step on a man's toe down there, it means that you're serious about him — I had no idea, I did it by mistake. So my father tells me I have to suffer the consequences and leave, or else

I would ruin his business negotiations — and he smelled from rubber, they all do down there — it's a beautiful country, they have gilded tables in the cafés and waiters dressed in red velvet who immediately ask you: *carabitchi* — that means: your name, please — and you tell them and they bring you a coffee pot with the guest's initials lit up on it.

That's the way you get to Lippi Wiesel's kind, because they need an international impression. I'm meeting him later.

I'm staying at Lippi Wiesel's. He believes that my father is with the government because that's the only sexual attraction I have for him, since his usual politics is blonde, and for men, politics and eroticism often go hand in hand because of race and conviction. I'm just glad that I got away from that Briekow woman. So they have courses teaching you foreign languages and ballroom dancing and etiquette and cooking. But there are no classes to learn how to be by yourself in a furnished room with chipped dishes, or how to be alone in general without any words of concern or familiar sounds.

I don't really like him all that much, but I'm with him, because every human being is like a stove for my heart that is homesick but not always longing for my parents' house, but for a real home — those are the thoughts I'm turning over in my mind. What am I doing wrong?

Perhaps I don't deserve better.

It's Christmas. The snow is making people drunk. Really drunk like wine. To be drunk is the only way not to get too old. So many years are crawling at me.

By way of Tilli, I sent Therese a bar of hazelnut chocolate, and I wish that her lonely wallpaper would develop many lips to give her passionate kisses.

To my mother, I gave a pot warmer via Therese by way of Tilli. For her, I wish that her husband, who is my father, would take her into his arms without being drunk.

I gave Tilli my own purple silk shirt and I wish that her Albert notices when she wears it, and that he finds work.

That Hulla was a whore. Maybe there's no grave for people like that and sometimes you make life on earth hell for people, and that's why it's stupid to be praying for them when they're finally happily dead. And when there're no men who pay, there won't be any Hullas — no man is allowed to say anything bad about that Hulla. I really wish her a heaven that has use for the good in her eyes. And when she's become an angel, she should have wings without any bandaids on them.

For myself, I so much wish for a voice of a man that's like a dark blue bell that says to me: Doris, listen to me; I'm telling you the right thing.

To my fur I give a waft of lavender perfume and wish that it won't lose its hair. And I wish that to everyone.

For Lippi Wiesel, I embroidered three picture frames with different kinds of flowers and I bought a Christmas tree and decorated it and locked it up in the bathroom. And then I'm going to light the candles, and I wish that we would think of each other as people.

I'm at a restaurant. I did Christmas. Christmas Eve. It's nothing but bullshit. I lit the candles and decorated the table with branches. And I'm waiting. And that Lippi doesn't show. Because I'm the kind of woman whose men are invited to a family on holidays, where it's boring, but they are on the same level and are considered society. And that's where he's celebrating, while my kind is waiting. And so I went to bed. There were candles on my tree and one of the branches went up in flames.

A great big red fire — I feel like having that kind of a fire — at school, there was Paul — we made a fire in the summer cottage, potato fire, and then we ate the burnt potato skins — Paul was the black bear, the sky was a steep gray mist — we built a tower out of one of the flames — I was the Indian with a chicken feather behind my ears, which stand out a bit but they hardly do that anymore now.

Besides, there's hair over them. I want a fire on crinkly hard earth.

"Forgive me, honey." There he is — that son of a bitch is drunk. "Forgive me, the Brennings wouldn't let me leave, I brought her fifteen marks-worth of orchids. Do you think that's enough? Her husband has connections, you know — she got two young Scotch terriers that we're going to feature in our photo section soon — unfortunately, they're not housetrained yet — see the stain on my knee — can you wash that out tomorrow?"

"You could at least turn on the radio," I say. *Silent night, holy night, all is calm, all is bright* — at school I was first soprano — *si-hi-lent night* —

"My dear girl, unfortunately I didn't get a gift for you, times are hard y'know, my little bug, they're cutting back everywhere. I didn't even get my last paycheck yet — what's Christmas anyway, all about business — but for you my child, I have a present for you, the most beautiful and the best I can give you — I give you me." And so he jumps on top of the bed, still wearing his shoes and suspenders.

"Please keep your clothes on, Sir," I say and I'm ashamed with rage.

"Our German Christmas," he pants, gasping for air.

"What about a German Christmas!" And I get out of bed — sleep with a drunkard, no way — I get my suitcase — "Just a minute, dear, I'm coming, I'm just looking for something" — keys on the table, thank God, hurry,

hurry — *silent night, holy* — where are the keys — *silent* . . . "I'm taking the soap, it's mine — bye!" — he's already asleep — be well!

And then I spent a winter night half-asleep in *Tiergarten* on a park bench. You can't imagine what that's like unless you've experienced it yourself.

3

A LOT OF WINTER AND A WAITING ROOM

I'm walking around with my suitcase and don't know what I want or where to go. I'm spending a lot of time at the waiting room at *Bahnhof Zoo*. Why is it that waiters are so full of spite, when you just so happen not to have any money?

I don't want to go home. I don't want to go to Tilli's. I don't want to go go Lippi's or to any of those other jerks — I don't want to anymore, I just don't want to. I don't want any men that get themselves invited for Christmas. I want — I want — what do I want?

There are waiting rooms and tables. That's where I sit. I don't want to pawn the fur. I refuse to — besides, I don't have any papers. Tilli knows a woman who would buy it.

But I don't want to sell. Sometimes my head just hits the tabletop in front of me, that's how heavy it is with fatigue. I continue to write because my hand wants something to do and my notebook with its white lined pages has a kind of readiness to receive my thoughts and my tiredness and to be a bed that my letters can lie in. That way at least part of me has a place to lie down.

And the table smells from cold ordinary cigarette ashes and *Maggi*'s seasoning and a restroom attendant gave me a meat sandwich that tasted like hygiene, which is the medical word for health. I know that because Rose Krall told me, who was also sitting at Jaedike's and whose boyfriend is a doctor. You can always tell the profession of a girl's last boyfriend, because they talk the language of his occupation.

My God, I'm so tired. And I don't feel like doing anything. It's all the same. The only thing that emerges from my fatigue is my curiosity about how things might continue — hello there, bring me another pint, will you? — why is there so much musical ado about the Rhine around here? There's someone playing the harmonica next door with his forehead as crumpled up as his life. And yesterday I was with a man who came on to me and took me for something that I'm not — that I'm not, even now. But there are whores standing around everywhere at night — so many of them around the *Alex*, so many, along the *Kurfürstendamm* and *Joachimsthaler Strasse* and at the *Friedrichstrasse* Station and everywhere. And they don't always look the part at all either, they walk in such a hesitant way. It's not always the face that makes a whore — I am looking into my mirror — it's the way they walk, as if their heart had gone to sleep.

So I was slowly walking past the Memorial Church, down the *Tauentzien*, walking farther and farther with an attitude of indifference in the backs of my knees and thus my walking was a kind of staying in place between wanting to walk further and a desire to walk back again, in that I really didn't want to do either. And then my body came to a stop at the corner, because corners create in one's back such a longing for contact with the sharp edge that is called a corner, and you want to lean up against them just once and feel them intensely. And you let the light that is coming from several streets illumine a face for you and you look at other faces and you wait. It's like a sport and full of tension.

I kept walking and walking, the whores were standing at corners plying their trade, and there was a sort of mechanism in me that duplicated precisely their walking and standing still. And then a man spoke to me, someone who thought himself my better, and I said, "I am not 'my child' to you, I am a lady."

And we talked to each other at a restaurant and I was supposed to order wine and I would much rather have had something to eat. But that's just like them — they don't mind paying large sums for something to drink, but as soon as they have to pay just a small amount for something to eat they feel taken advantage of, because food is a necessity, but having a drink is superfluous and therefore elegant. He had a dueling scar on his face and was looking for the Berlin underworld. Because he was an out-of-towner wanting to have some danger, so he could show courage.

So I took the Scarface to a basement behind *Nollendorfplatz* — and it was completely empty in there. And in the middle there was room to dance and a dreary flame plus that mirror of a foggy moon reflected in a puddle in the backyard. And it had high ceilings and was cold and cheap. On the walls were pictures of people in the old days doing immoral things. Some of the tables had tablecloths on them like a caretaker would do on Sundays. Hookers were wearing dresses that were fashionable five years ago or longer. Completely out of style and dead Middle Ages, like in those novels. And a band. It was a one-man show and he gets one mark per night. He had been in jail and before that he had been an actor. He looked like those young heroes at my old theater, with their blond hair and their faces a color that made them look like babies under the stage lighting and like those sick old men at the hospital during the day. He had also written for newspapers. So now he's standing in the middle of the empty gray space holding a bag made from news-paper. And he sticks it on his nose and lights the tip of it. Boom-boom makes the band and then the lights go off, which only makes you realize that they had been on in the first place. He kneels down with the newspaper bag burning like a flame on his nose — and he bends over backwards — he's wearing those Tyrolean pants.

"What do you want to drink?" the Scarface asks. "There's nothing happening here."

The hooker with the red face claps and an echo of hers claps too. The bag is very large, it's burning slowly. The actor is shaking the flames off his face — *O Donna Clara* plays the band and the dark light comes back on. His name is Herbert, I know him. Three years ago he was still one of the elite. And then he puts on a tiny idiotic hat and makes faces.

"Give him one mark," I tell the Scarface.

"A penny is plenty," he says, and throws Herbert a nickel.

"Too bad you didn't have anything smaller," I say.

Then conversation. It's always about sex. You really get tired of it. Jokes about sex, stories about sexual con-quests, lectures on serious science about sex, which is supposed to sound like an expert discussion which is why it tends to get even more disgusting. But you're not sup-posed to show your disgust, because if you do, the Scarface will give you this condescending smile: pooh-pooh, I thought you were a woman who's above that, but women always have a dirty mind.

So last night I slept a few hours in a cab. The cabdriver didn't ask for money. "I have to stay here anyway," he said, "make yourself comfortable. If I have to drive someone, I'll wake you. But there won't be anyone, with the way business is these days."

I curled up and slept, and he left me alone. Until there were stars in the sky, but it was morning already, but still at night. And the light oozed from the earth like silken white fog, and my tired head wondered how it was possible that it could come out of such hard pavement. The sky didn't have any light in it. My back hurt.

"Thank you," I said to the cabdriver and I held my hand out to him which was all warm and sticky and prickly from lying on the upholstery.

"Morning," he says, and doesn't touch it.

So I left. He was all closed up and there was no room for a thank-you in him. And it was then that I knew what it means to be lucky — lucky to have met a person during those three minutes of the day that he's good. Because I have a lot of time on my hands — you can imagine that that adds up. There are 24 hours in a day, and half of that is night. That leaves you with 12. And that's 12 times 60 minutes, that is, 720 minutes minus three minutes of goodness still leaves you with 717 minutes worth of nasty ordinary person. You have to be aware of that if you don't want to let it get you down. Everybody has a right to be nasty, after all. I would love to have my hair washed, then I would have hair like an Indian. "You hair is like the eternal forest," someone said to me once — who was that? Forests. That makes me think of blueberries and small metal buckets. They used to have red cabbage in them. Oh, here's Karl.

I just had an interesting conversation, thanks to Karl. He's a character. Planting lettuce and radishes and making small pipes out of wood and little dolls. And he's living in a cottage colony and he's a real Berliner with his cheeky dialect and brassy ash-blond hair and always in a good mood. He used to work as a fitter, but now he's out of work and still young. And he makes a lot of odd little things that he carries around with him on a vendor's tray and radishes and stuff like that, and he says he's a Woolworth on legs, rain or shine. And he sells his stuff in the *Westend* and sometimes he has a quick beer at the *Bahnhof Zoo* waiting room.

"Hi there, Siberian girl," he calls out to me. "Why that fur coat? Come with me, help me a little, work with me."

His mouth is damn hungry for a woman.

"What should I work with you on, Karl?" I ask.

"There are two small rooms in my cottage," he says, "and there's a goat you can milk. You can make our bed, wash the windows, clean, sew eyes onto colorful little dolls — come on girl, you have such a cute face and all the rest — do you want to become a hooker? Believe me, there's a hell of a lot of competition among those who want to work. But there's even more competition among those who don't want to work, among whores and those who want to be somebody without any effort and hard work — why would you want to be where the competition is worst?"

Albert's been arrested for burglary. Tilli for helping him. He was drinking at a bar. And bragging. And the silver fork sticking out of his pocket. And there's a police officer in the back of the room. I can only look down on so much stupidity. Are these real criminals? No, they're not.

Gay Gustav is sitting at my table looking like a piece of pukey shit. He's sitting there sleeping. And then come the police. I take off. They take Gustav with them to the police station. His head is still asleep while he walks. I hide with the restroom attendant.

"Frau Molle," I say, "I'll make it up to you some day."

"I don't believe that someone can get back on his feet once he's started to slide," she says and just stares at me.

I force myself to make conversation with her. All I want is talk, talk, talk — she has a small space heater. "It's warm in here, Frau Molle." There are small lacquered tiles that are like a mirror for my voice.

"This winter hasn't been cold at all," she says.

"Yes," I say.

And then I sit down again and continue writing, all befuddled. Gustav is back. The police let him go. So he walked back and sank down in the corner and is asleep again. And he's so tired that he forgets to be gay. When you're that hungry and tired, you become normal again.

"You're still sitting here," says Karl and orders me a beer and some wieners. "Will you come with me?" he asks.

"No," I say. "I have ambition" — with those wieners in my stomach, I'm ambitious again.

"What do you mean, ambition? That's nonsense," he says rolling his voice. "You think I'm still ambitious? Food, drink, sleep, a nice girl, a good mood — that's my ambition. And if I can get that through honest work and honest effort, I'm fine. And if I can't, I steal, I get something for myself to eat and I have only a guilty conscience, if I'm stupid enough to get caught."

And so he tells me about socialism. "I don't think it'll be beautiful, but perhaps we'll have real air to breathe, and it's at least a start — right now, all we have is a big mess. Will you come with me? Well then, don't — you can kiss my ass with your ambition."

"Your butt isn't too bad either," I say. "And thanks for the wieners."

"Do you want to come to the club with me?" asks that little Schanewsky.

So I go to the club behind *Alexanderplatz*. He pays for my ticket. Just happens to have work. It's a proletarian club. Only little Schanewsky and four girls are there that night. Two rooms on the fourth floor, lots of books, and those topsy-turvy letters on the walls in a Jewish language.

I'm talking to the girl who is a worker. She's called Else and has delicate skin.

I rest my head on her shoulder. They are talking to each other and I understand nothing, nothing at all. There are enormous things going on in the world, and I have no idea. It's stupid. But their voices are like a sleepy hum to me, Else's shoulder smells like mother, there's white paper on the tables and the light is that of a kitchen. I'm starting to doze off. Schanewsky offers me a dish made from chopped liver and onions — I'm sleeping and dreaming that I eat. And the voices are humming and I'm thinking that I have to tell them that I'm not into politics — you always have to be something. And it's always about politics. And always something else.

There are round oranges and cheese and meat on the buffet.

And then Else's shoulder slides away from under me and there's noise — shoes, lots of shoes were coming — the girls were screaming and throwing the windows open. Schanewsky's eyes were looking softly at me from the corner — the room burst with ten blond windbreakers — they are their enemies and again it's got something to do with politics. And they threw themselves at the buffet and under that kitchen lighting they looked pale and starved and they threw the oranges on the floor and ate all the sausages. And made a tired ruckus. And stuffed down all the sausages. And then they left. What was that all about?

Every day is really the start of a new year, but today a New Year is beginning in a special way, because it's New Year's Eve. You drink punch and watch the fireworks. It's complete rubbish, but nonetheless my heart is heavy because I'm without anything colorful and without warmth and all that. Bars are out. I'm going to go around to several restaurants to sell flowers tomorrow. Okay, I'm going to let someone talk to me and whatever else and take the money. Just once, and never again. I would just love to go to the movies again.

"Do you want to come with me?"

"Yes."

And his voice is like dark green moss. But what does that really mean? How would I know how a sex killer talks, do I know how those, whose name I won't put on paper, talk? A huge creature of a bus was running past us with streamers hanging down from it. I was curious to look into the eyes of the Green Moss — it was New Year's Eve and the ground was all slippery. And for the past three minutes it had been 1932.

And that's the main thing about a new year: at the office, you have to type a new date on the letters, which is easy to forget during the first four weeks.

"Poor gigolo, beautiful gigolo," the Green Moss was singing.

"Why?" I ask.

"My wife left me."

"Berlin is a big city where lots of things are happening," I say, because you have to say something when men confide in you, even though you usually say the wrong thing, which is why it doesn't matter what you say. So now I'm sitting in the shelter of an apartment.

"Your wife will come back," I say — with my kind of luck.

We go out into the street. I can see the Moss's eyes — nice blue color, colorfast.

"Yes, I'll come with you." Ten marks — I'm going to ask him for ten marks. And his lower lip looks like that of a sensual crybaby. God, those guys move you so quickly.

"You're just passing through town?" he asks. Stupid ass. Okay, so I'm just passing through. I am carrying a suitcase — genuine vulcanized fiber — a suitcase with my *Bemberg* shirts and stuff, with my hard-earned Berlin things. If he takes off with my suitcase, I'll bite his head off.

"I'm so lonely," he says. They all are. So what?

"I don't know where to go," I say to him on the *Tauentzien* and my knees caved in a little, because I was so hungry and on purpose.

"Hey, hey, hey, so you'll come with me!" Okay, Green Moss. And we get on the bus — not even a taxi?

"Poor little girl," he says. On the bus, I get overwhelmed by pity, and I cry my eyes out. Damn. "Where are we going?"

"To my place."

There's a scale in the bathroom. I weigh 97 pounds. My ribs are sticking out — if fuller figures become fashionable again, I'm in real trouble. I had such a stupid scratching in my throat. I was coughing, too. And it was the apartment of summer for me.

It's always such a strange feeling to stand in front of a door when someone else opens it and in a strange apartment building. The marble smells so cold and doesn't like me. And the rightful tenant turns on the light, knowing exactly where it is — that gives him the upper hand. Then you go up in a small room that is an elevator — with such God-awful mirrors on each side — am I really that ugly? And you're embarrassed because you're never elegant enough — but I almost didn't care anymore. He was wearing a coat made from a thick gray material called Ulster. Ulster is always gray. I'm thinking, sex killers always wear windbreakers. Then the elevator comes to a stop and almost makes you throw up. And then one has respect for a person who has a key chain that makes a clinking sound and is such a mystery of many keys, only one person knows it. And there you stand, powerless. He wears his hair parted in the middle. He's blond and neat in a completely uninteresting way.

"Please," he says. And I go in before he does. Everything is very modern. Not this heavy oak you find at the industrialists.

"I'm very glad you're here. I mean, I'm glad anyone is here. What I have experienced is funny for others, but it's not at all funny to me. That's what separates me from others."

"Yes, yes," I say.

Would you like to stay a little while, Miss — ?"

"Doris," I say.

"Miss Doris," says he.

So he has an apartment with cork flooring, three rooms and a bath, a rubber-tree plant, and a divan, so wide, with a silk cover and fine steel dentist office lamps — he has everything and yet he howls and moans about some woman who's taken off. But there are so many of them. He has a lacquer bed, so smooth, and little night tables like Japanese hay boxes and rings around his eyes because of a woman. And there are hordes of us walking from *Alexanderplatz* to the Memorial Church and from the *Tauentzien* to *Friedrichstrasse*. And there are pretty ones, and elegant ones. Young ones too. And there are hordes of men running around — should I be worried about why I'm getting that one and not the other one, if I have something to eat? It's all the same in the end — I'm making an exception for odd-balls, like extremely deaf and dumb ones, cripples or sadists. Mister, you idiot, whatever one of them has, the other one has too. And I was allowed to eat three giant oranges.

What a wet rag — "Cold hands?" Well, how the hell should they get warm? No, please, I want him to let go of my hands — it disgusts me. This moss-like voice and this soft ado about my hands.

"Tired, tired girl — tired, poor little woman. You must have been through a lot, haven't you? Well, don't be sad any more — do you want to tell me? How old are you?"

"Eighteen." Tell him? I don't want to tell him. Not a word.

"Why such big sad eyes?" Always a voice like moss, like a delicate plant — my God, no — if he continues to care that much about me, I'm going to kick his shin. He turns me off. It's disgusting to me that he's so good to me. I'm feeling this strong urge to say something nasty.

"Let's go to bed."

Okay, let's go to bed. I go to the bathroom. I take my clothes off. There's a large mirror. Is that me? Yes, it's me all right. My left leg is wider than my right one. There's no meat on my bones and my skin is yellow and incredibly tired. I look like a starved goat. My face is the size of a small cup and all squooshed and I have a pimple on my chin —

something like this wants to become a star — something like this — what a joke. I bit into the bathtub, that's how angry I was. Greasy hair, all messed up — one, two, three ribs — hip bones sticking out — God, that's what a skeleton looks like — that teaches you, that teaches you, gentlemen. And under circumstances that you're supposed to be sensual. I want to throw up. He has to give me ten marks, I'll take him only once. He disgusts me so much, I don't want him — ten marks, and then I'll go sell flowers, then — I'll also buy myself some cold cream for my face — I — if I keep looking at myself in the mirror, I'm going to go down in price. Enough. Where's my Bemberg silk nightgown? Ten marks.

"I made your bed on the sofa."

I guess that's okay, too. Bed or sofa, who cares. And perhaps I won't have to leave right after and can stay here until tomorrow morning — but I can't look at him, I don't want him next to me afterward — you disgusting, soft frog-like creature. He strokes my head — please don't, please don't, I can't, I don't want to — ten marks! — and there's a scream at the bottom of my throat. "Please stop stroking my hair. I can't have that" — to want to be good to me now, that's really too much.

"I'm so tired," I say. A bed. To lie in for a long time.

"Good night," he says, "sleep tight."

And he's gone! And is not coming back. At first I'm surprised, then I'm ashamed. Then I'm thinking, who knows what particularly disgusting strategy this is. But it's fine by me. Then I fall asleep. Had interesting dreams, but can't remember them unfortunately. And today I did almost nothing but sleep and hardly ate anything, only slept. And I don't remember much of the words that happened, I only remember my sleep.

"I made coffee for you," he says this morning at eight o'clock. "I'm going to the office now. You just sleep in. I'll be back at six o'clock. Are you still going to be here?"

"Yes."

"There's food in the pantry. You can take whatever you want."

"Yes."

Yes, I'm going to be here. Where else should I be? But I'm so mad — you stupid Moss, I'm gonna figure you out.

"Could you leave some cigarettes for me?" I ask.

"I'll leave the box on the coffee table." Wow, he's smoking those at six marks — well, all right. If he can afford it. And by noon, I've smoked all of them.

So I ask him: "Listen, you don't know me at all, but you let me stay here all day long. I could trash your place or carry everything out."

He looks at me like: "First of all, I wouldn't care. And secondly, you wouldn't do it anyway." Of course I wouldn't — but why not care?

"I guess you don't really have to work for it, do you?"

"Sure."

"What do you do?"

He's in advertising. And leaves the house at eight in the morning and comes home at six or seven o'clock. His face is wrinkled and leathery and under the eyes his skin is a grayish blue. And he's 37. That's still pretty young for a guy.

I'm still tired and sleeping all the time and still not enough. My arms are just hanging down at my sides and I don't feel like doing anything at all. And I don't have any desire — for nothing, not money, not my mother, not Therese. I get out of bed and there's the coffee. He put a coffee warmer over it that's colorful and crocheted and has "good family" written all over it. It's twelve noon and the coffee is lukewarm. And there are rolls and good butter and sticky honey. I eat only a little. Sometimes my eyes wake up and it's eight in the morning, and then he walks back and forth and sits at the coffee table across from me. "Just keep sleeping," he says.

So I continue to sleep. And then it's twelve noon and I bathe, but not to be elegant but because I can't lie in bed all the time, and so the hot tub becomes my next bed. And then I move my feet to the room with the desk and I sit there and write a little and then I lie down on the chaise longue and all of a sudden I'm lying down again and I'm asleep again. And then he comes home. And he straightens up the apartment and says nothing — perhaps I should be doing that, but I don't care if he kicks me out. I'll just lie on the street and continue to sleep. Then we sit down and there's food on the table and bread and ham. And he has a glass of cognac. I don't want any.

"Why do you let me stay here?" I ask him.

"Because I'm afraid to come home and there's nobody there who breathes — please stay."

This is complete craziness — now he's begging me to stay.

Last night he starts asking questions about me. What can I tell him? Right now, I don't know any words about myself.

It just seemed too ominous. I'm having three cognacs and then I turn on the radio — there's strange Rome and music. And on the wall across from me is a black and white picture, a profile. And the wall is painted yellow like an afternoon in August. The picture is moving. The flooring is cork and there's a small balcony. You freeze immediately, the moment you step on the balcony and it's winter — and such a joy to be warm in a summery apartment.

"Don't you want to go for a walk? Don't you want to go to the movies sometimes? What do you do all day long?"

"Sleep."

"You're still tired, Miss Doris?"

"Yes."

"Are you ill?"

"No."

"You have to eat more. You have to get some fresh air!"

"Yes."

"Why do you never laugh? Are you grieving? Did somebody do something terrible to you?" The picture is moving.

"Mister," I say, getting up, "you let me just sleep here. You let me eat and you put a crocheted hat over the coffee-pot every morning, and a box of cigarettes at six — I owe you — if you, if you want something from me — well then" — Is he saying anything? "I mean, I have to pay you somehow."

"Well, if you like, Miss Doris, you can make the beds and straighten up a bit tomorrow."

Maybe I'm so ugly he doesn't want me?

Going for a walk all by yourself is terribly boring. But now I'm hungry. And I did the dishes and set the table. But I'm not making his bed. That's disgusting. His bedroom turns me off.

He puts ten marks next to the coffee cup. Does he want me to leave? Is that what this means? He doesn't say a word, just puts it there. I just don't get it with him. It grosses me out, to walk so softly and speak so softly and never be reasonable. So I'm just going to go out and buy pork chops. I'll fry them up for tonight with Brussels sprouts, so he'll get a warm meal for a change.

"You're a man," I'm going to tell him, "you have to eat meat. You have to sink your teeth into it. Right now you're a silly plant. That's what happens if you don't eat meat."

Now he's messing around in his room next door. For crying out loud, why don't you just take the bone with your hands, I want to tell him — since it's just the two of us. It's all nice and well to be a cavalier, but you're like a plant.

"Dear little Doris, I thank you."

For what, you stupid asparagus? You — please stop talking like that. And he should just pick up that bone. He really should. He always has such clean white hands — hands have to be dirty sometimes. I would just love to break one of his nails.

"Please," I say, "I can type. You can dictate your letters to me," I tell him, and so he dictates.

I put flowers on the table, because it looks nice. But now he's going to say again: "Oh dear little Doris," and behave like overcooked asparagus. It's better to throw the flowers out of the window.

Yesterday he tells me: "Little Doris, you ran away from home, I think — let's write to your parents. I'm sure they're worried — you silly girl, didn't you know what could have happened to you here in Berlin?"

"Do you have any idea what has already happened to me!" say my guts, but not my mouth. So he thinks I'm innocent. Which explains a lot. Because at first Hubert hadn't wanted to either — because of the responsibility. Does it really make such a difference?

So he's drinking his cognac and says: "Women like to run away, don't they? Women just can't stand it anymore, can they? My wife — " and he tells me about his wife. And that tells me he really considers me innocent and coming from a good family. I do speak very little and in an educated manner. "I'm tired," I say — and what education would let you say that any differently? "Thank you," I say, "please," I say — what education would make a difference when saying those words? And so he makes me into something incredible, or else he wouldn't be talking to me like that about his wife. That's the kind he is. A plant. And he shows me her picture. It kills me that she's pretty. What do you mean blonde? He's blond himself, so he should be more interested in the dark type.

"She has a cute face."

"How old is she?" I ask.

"Twenty-seven." What an old cow. "Can you imagine, Miss Doris, that she had a brain like a real strong woman's body? She was so honest — and it was as if she were taking her clothes off, and you just had to love her for that. And her lies were like light sheer colorful fabric and you could see her body right through it — her lies were so honest that you had to love them too. . . ."

Why didn't that bitch wear an undershirt under those light clothes, I think to myself — he's talking like those novels of the elite. It really doesn't make a difference whether a man is writing novels or whether he's in love.

"You see, I'm away all day, and she's waiting for me — she used to be a dancer — there was so much imagination in her movements. So she goes out in the afternoon and I say: "Just go, do anything you enjoy, go dancing, my darling, here's some money, go to the teas." And there's a young poor gigolo, a beautiful gigolo, which he hadn't always been. He came. Used to be an actor. Before that an engineer. And she's artistic too. And very ambitious. And he treats her badly."

"That's it," I say, "this soft way of not wanting to, and to treat her well on top of that. That's too much for a woman."

He always tried to spare her, he says. Can you show me a woman who can take that kind of consideration for months on end? It's making me sick. "I would have run away from you too," I tell him.

"Really," he says and looks at me with his questioning blue eyes — "and I don't know anything about women, I — "

That moved me again, much against my own will. His elbows on the table, his hair blond, ash blond the way men are, not really blond. And music from Rome and leathery skin and two toothbrushes dyed black — those are his eyebrows. And in front of him porcelain dishes with mandarin oranges, those are simple oranges — not as sour and easier to peel. Of course he has mandarin oranges. He likes to keep things simple.

"You should eat oranges," I shout at him. But mandarin oranges are easier. Music from the radio. Is he sleeping now? I'm sure he wears striped flannel pajamas. So she ran away.

"I always did my duty," he says. As if that were enough. He's big and tall. Does he have a skinny back? He should be eating lard, lard from a goose.

I happened to know a joke that wasn't obscene. Why don't you laugh for a change, Green Moss, everyone has to laugh sometimes!

"You have a talent for storytelling," he says.

"I was on my way to the stage," I say.

"My wife wanted to dance at *Charell's*," he says.

"I know him personally," I say. Later on I remember it's not true.

"Please give me some money." He gives it to me.

"Do you need velvet? My wife used to wear blue velvet — "

I bought a goose.

"Are you sure it's fresh? It doesn't smell?" I ask.

"If you always smell as good as that beast, you can consider yourself lucky," complains the market vendor who wears a black scarf around her neck.

"Let's not talk about my smell, let's talk business," I'm quick to let her know.

And I fried him a goose. On Sunday and with my own hands. And goose lard is good for the nerves in your back, my mother used to say.

"May I?" he says elegantly and he takes a drumstick in his hands.

"I hope you like it," I say.

I had a little bit of breast too. And we have enough for the next few days. I think he liked it. So he starts up again: about his wife and that she had such long legs and you always had to be worried about her. So what? I bought a measuring tape. How long do legs have to be? His name is Ernst. What a joke. Ernst. Can you imagine. . . . "Why do you smile, Mona Lisa?"

"Nice song, isn't it?" I ask, in an effort to continue our elegant conversation after dinner.

"My wife loved Tchaikovsky," he says.

"Really — I used to know a guy called Rannovsky, you know, he had a hook where 'kovsky' ends — and there was a Hulla — "

"What do you know about life," he says. Enough. You imagine your answers, but you don't say them. It's all the same. Nobody would understand anyway.

"See that cushion over there? My wife embroidered it."

Yes, I can see the cushion, when you buy cigarettes at four, you get these embroidered flowers in each pack-

147

age — if you smoke, you don't have to embroider, do you? And he tells me all those strange things and always talks about his wife and what times we have nowadays. Everything is being torn up and destroyed and if you want to be honest, you have to admit that you can't figure things out anymore. And particularly an educated man can't build anything for himself anymore, and everything is uncertain. The whole world is uncertain and life and the future and what we used to believe in and what we believe in now, and work isn't fun anymore, because you always have a bad conscience because there are so many people who don't have any. And so a man has nothing but his wife and he's very dependent on her because he wants to be able to believe in something, and that's the love for his wife — and then she doesn't want all that love and that way you're not worth anything at all anymore. And because you're nothing but a burden on humanity these days — that's why you need that special someone so badly to whom you can be a joy. And then all of a sudden you're no joy anymore. And true elegance is disappearing in this day and age and in times like that, women are the first ones to slide, and men are held by the law and they hold women too — and once all the laws of humanity have disappeared, man has nothing more to hold onto, but you can't tell, because he never did in a moral sense — and what falls first in a way to be noticed by everyone, that's always the woman.

And I try to remember everything he says and I want to think about it, but I don't have a real understanding. At first, I wanted to do a symbol from time to time, like at home, but then all I said was: "Yes, there are a lot of whores around these days," but I don't really know if there are more of them than there used to be and why everyone is always talking about our times. When you're a small child and you're just beginning to understand, all you hear about are those terrible times and what is going to happen. And when I think of time, all I can think of is that I'm going to be old and ugly and all shriveled up, but I can't believe that — but that's the only horrible thing about time for me.

And: "My wife was able to sing with a light high-pitched voice."

"So I sing — *Das ist die Liebe der Matrosen* — the most wonderful song there is."

"Schubert," he says. Why? "She used to sing like Schubert composed." *Das ist die Liebe der Matrosen* — that's some piece of shit of a song, isn't it? What about Schubert, what does that mean? *Das ist die Lie* — straight from life, as my mother used to say about a good movie.

And I did make his bed.

On his night table that looks like a Japanese haybox are books. Baudelaire. I'm sure that's French. But in German. Lesbos, island of withering nights. That tells you everything. I know what they're talking about here — that's almost obscene. Withering nights! Lesbos! That gives you some insight into men and into Berlin as well.

There are bars with women wearing shirts with stiff necks and ties and they are terribly proud to be perverts, as if that weren't something nobody can do anything about. I always used to say to Therese: "I'm happy that I have such large eyes but they were given to me, that's why I can't be proud of them." But those perverts, they're proud of it. There's one of those bars in *Marburger Strasse*. Some men seem to like it. Is he that kind? And I didn't want to read that Van de Velde either when Therese gave me the book. When you write these things down, they become obscene.

Lesbos, island of — thank God there are no pictures.

There's a bottle of lavender on his bedside table. His sheets are straight and quiet. Doesn't he move in his sleep? And his towels are so clean and his toothpaste. How disgusting could it be to brush your teeth with his toothbrush?

What am I going to cook today? There's still that leftover goose. We've got to get our money's worth. You have to economize. There'll be baked apples for dessert and a bouillion for starters. The spoons for the soup are for real-they're stamped.

I run the vacuum cleaner — sssss, I'm a thunderstorm. It just so happens I break the wife's picture. They had so many words in common, he says — there are these small tender memories that are seemingly uneventful. Me:

"She's gone and you have to start directing your thoughts elsewhere."

Him: "I don't have any more joy. Why am I alive, whom do I work for?"

"I bet you never had to live through really tough times."

"Yes, I did," he says. Well, I'm not going to ask what he considers tough times. There are those who already feel sorry for themselves when they haven't had a hot meal by three in the afternoon.

I make an attempt. "What are you writing all the time?" he asks.

"I'm writing about my experiences."

"Really?" Not another word. He could ask a little more.

He tells me how he met his wife and that she's very ambitious and wanted to be in the world and her art, and how she became more and more restless every day and crazy and afraid to grow old and to have been nothing but the wife of a man in a small apartment. And no independence and no life's work. And one night they both went to see a Spanish Argentinian dancer and for three days she was ill, that's how jealous she was, and she had to stay in bed. And at first she didn't want him at all, because she wasn't well and she wanted to do things on her own and with her own strength. That's quite a drama she must have put on for him. That kind of man will believe anything. It's no fun lying to him — he'll believe anything you tell him. I need more of a challenge. He's too easy. After all, I've developed my lying into an art form. He doesn't ask me any questions anymore. But he did notice that I thoroughly cleaned the house. Tomorrow I'm going to wash the curtains, because of all that smoke.

"Herr Schlappweisser," I say to the street vendor," I want two smoked herrings, with roe." I'm going to make that into caviar. Caviar is supposed to stimulate. His herrings are gigantic, and otherwise he's a nice person too.

"Young lady, this is the best of the best. Your husband will enjoy them." His mother has open legs, he told me once.

"How is your mother, Herr Schlappweisser?"

"Thank you so much for asking, Madam."

"How's business? Are you suffering much from the emergency legislation?"

"Well, times are sh — "

"May I also have a flounder please," I interrupt, to prevent him from saying a word I don't want to hear.

So I'm walking down *Kaiserallee* with my fur coat and my smoked fish, two of them with caviar in their bellies, when a guy accosts me. "You're making an enormous mistake talking to me that way," I say. Not another word. With a regal gesture, I cut off any further conversation. By the way, I will definitely have to take in his black shoes tomorrow.

And so I make another attempt. I put my notebook on the coffee table and pretend to be asleep by eight. He looks at it — I can feel the blood pulsing in my knees — and then he pushes it aside without looking at it again. That's incredibly civilized, I think, but maybe he's just not interested in anything.

"You're so lovely, Miss Doris, how do I deserve this? Is there anything I can do for you? Do you have a wish I can fulfill?" But I've got everything.

"You don't look good," I say to him, "Tonight you're going to bed at ten."

"Oh, but I can't sleep anyway," he moans.

So I get mad. "Stop imagining things. That's a lie that you can't sleep at night because of all your troubles. When I can hear you snoring next door every night." I so want to give him my notebook — I want to be a real person — he should read my book — I work for him, I cook for him, I'm Doris — Doris isn't just some piece of dirt. I don't want to be innocent, I want to be the real Doris here and not that silly civilized product of the Green Moss's imagination.

I've gained five pounds. Slowly I'm regaining my allure.

He's stopped stroking my hair.

I have a lot of work to do. I'm in charge of the entire household.

And then we have to get some fresh air every day, so we go for a walk after dinner every night. It's evening and none of the doors are open anymore. There are a few stars in the sky and my stomach feels calm. People are walking their dogs in elegant streets. It's very nice. We make conversation. Some nights we don't talk at all, and those are the best. That's when I have a few moments without effort. He hates war. I tell him of the man who gave me the colorful beaded necklace, the one who had lost his eyesight and who had grown old in the war. And then he tells me about the little grenade splinter that's wandering around in his shoulder. "Here — feel it," and he puts his hand on his shirt while we are under a large tree without leaves. It was very interesting.

"Does it hurt?" I ask.

"No."

And there are lots of old men around selling matches and shoelaces — so many of them — and everywhere there are whores in the streets, and young men with starved voices. We always give everyone ten cents, that's so little, and sometimes I lose interest in being happy. And then we go home. Sometimes you feel like you want to hug a lamppost.

"Watch out," he says, "there's a step."

"Close your mouth, there's a draft at this corner," I say.

And I make coffee in the morning. I get up too, now. But it was so nice of him to always put that crocheted cover over the coffeepot. I look at the clock — I used to have a watch, the one from Gustav Mooskopf, but it's broken — I don't really need one. But I want him to know about me. I'm going to give him my book tomorrow.

In the morning, he polishes his shoes in the kitchen. He would always polish mine as well. Did he love his wife that much? I guess you always experience the man's previous woman in a man.

I washed his combs, mended three pairs of socks, and read in that funny book on his bedside table — I see your virgin urges manifest themselves, I see your joy and lost happiness — my spirit appears multiplied, indulges in all your sins and my soul returns all your virtues . . . nobody can understand that, but it rhymes.

I can't imagine ever calling him Ernst.

I did it. I gave him my book. We're sitting at the table, covered with a shiny, smoothed-out-with-thumbnails, yellow and white tablecloth with a pattern on it — "Do you like patterns? Please don't have any cognac."

I would love to powder my face, that would give me more courage. I guess it's okay to put on lipstick. The color is going to stay on until tomorrow morning, until I wash it off. Sometimes I have this funny empty feeling in my arms. It's embarrassing, that feeling. But it's not all that important.

"Do you want to listen to foreign radio?"

"My wife — she never loved anyone before me," he says.

Please, keep your mouth shut. All of that belongs to your wife. You're a beast, you, you're like they all are — it's so mean — you're just like all those other guys at the bar, sitting there like a plucked chicken — for a moment, I felt friendship for his wife. I can't explain — please, how can I tell him, how?

"You can talk about your love and your feeling and your desires — but please, you must not talk about the love of another woman, you're not allowed to do that." That's what I told him.

So he laughs. "I'm just so glad whenever I can talk about her," he says. Am I a Therese for him? I'm sick of his wife. Therese always wanted me to talk about my men. There's a difference, isn't there?

So we sit. Sometimes we laugh, and there's music on the radio, and yellow patterns. "Have you ever met a more boring guy in your life, Miss Doris?" I wonder why he calls me "Miss" sometimes, and sometimes he doesn't.

"I've experienced every possible kind of guy," I answer.

"Well, well!"

"Would you like to read in my book?"

"Yes."

And we sit on what has been my bed all this time. It's like someone going through my guts. I feel sick. Like an overinflated balloon. I smoke a cigarette — I'm going to throw up — his hair, which isn't really blond, because he's a man, under the light — Tilli used to wash hers with chamomile tea — "Please don't read the last pages!" He's flipping back and forth. I'm afraid to look at his face — if only I hadn't — "Please don't read past New Year's — my voice is bulging out of my mouth — and I see your blissful days and your lost happiness — I wonder what he's reading right now. I don't really care — too bad I can't see his face — well, I guess you're going to have to leave my pure home — I'm going to take all the stamped silver spoons with me, I promise. I wanted to make fried kidneys tomorrow — at the thought of kidneys I lose it and shed a tear. Thank God I didn't really do it with the Onyx, at least that's one less. I also didn't do it with the Red Moon — but I stole the shirts. It's okay for him to know. Only those passages where I was really depressed, I wish I could cover those up. Those where I was a bitch, well all right. But those instances where I was different, that's all so embarrassing, it's digging into my stomach — my face is all puffed up like a red tomato — I don't understand how people can write books that everyone in the world can read — please stop, please — "Have you gotten to New Year's yet — please, are you at New Year's — why don't you say something — whether you — "

"Just a minute," he says.

I have this flea bite under my left foot that's itching like hell, and I so much want to take my shoe off — they always get you where a decent person is not supposed to scratch herself, those bastards. The sole of your left foot isn't too bad, actually. "Have you gotten to New Year's yet?" — ammonia would be perfect — "Do we have any ammonia around the house, for heaven's sake?"

"My dear little Doris, you're not crying, are you?"

Stop imagining my weaknesses, Sir, will you?

"Well, I'm glad you came to me just in time," he says.

Boy oh boy, I just love that music they're playing on the radio.

"Shall we go for a walk, Miss Doris?"

"Yes."

"Watch out, Doris, there's a step here."

"Please keep your mouth shut at this drafty corner, Mister." And at the big tree without leaves, a fox terrier is lifting up his leg. Oh!

So we had a heart-to-heart talk. Are people who work more ethical than people who don't work?

"You know what we're going to do, Miss Doris? We're going to return your fur coat and make sure you get your papers, and then we're going to get you work." That's what he says.

Forget it! As if someone like me, who has no education and no foreign language skills except for olala and has no high school diploma and nothing could get anywhere through work. And no knowledge of foreign currencies and opera and all the rest of it. And no degrees. And no chance to get more than 120 in an honest way —

and to always be typing files and more files, so boring, without any motivation and no risk to win or lose. And just more of that nonsense with commas and foreign words and all that. And all that effort to learn — but it's so much, too much, it overwhelms me and won't fit into my head and everything is spinning around me. There's nobody you can ask and teachers are expensive. You have 120 marks with deductions to turn in at home or live on. You're hardly worth more, but are hardly satisfied in spite of it. And you want a few nice clothes, because at least then you're no longer a complete nobody. And you also want a coffee once in a while with music and an elegant peach melba in very elegant goblets — and that's not at all something you can muster alone, again you need the big industrialists for that, and you might as well just start turning tricks. Without an eight-hour day. And if you're really lucky, you become like Therese. You sit there and you save, and you eat very little. And you have a love. You take your savings book and you buy dresses so you will be beautiful, after all he's something better. And you won't take any money from him for love, so he won't get the wrong idea. And then you're with him at night — and in love and all that — and at eight in the morning you're back in the office. And you're over 20 and your face is getting ruined from all that work and love, because people need to get sleep. But he loves you, which is why it doesn't really matter to you. You end it a hundred times and then you wait terribly — please come back, it doesn't matter, please come back, and you buy expensive facial creams. You have this fatigue. His wife is sleeping at home. Sometimes she worries, but she can sleep in and gets enough money, because of his bad conscience. That's when they get very generous. Therese's room is cold and ugly and his apartment is nice and warm. She's crying a lot because of her nerves, and a man gets sick of that — "My dear child, we have to break up, I'm destroying your life, you have other opportunities, I'm being eaten up with suffering but I have to leave you. You'll find another one you can marry, you're still pretty." And that still is killing you. Good-bye — blablabla — the dresses have gone out of fashion, you won't buy new ones and you eat little and you save. And you keep this devout smile on your face in front of your boss, that jerk whom you should hate even if he's good to you, because he could dismiss you.

And you're getting old early, at a time when a star in her ermine coat hasn't aged at all yet — you have your Doris who experiences great things until she too has become a Therese. That's the way it goes with Therese and with so many others, now I know. I won't play along with that, you can fuck yourselves —. Compared to that, a whore's life is more interesting. At least she's got her own business.

"Dear Mr. Ernst, I don't want to work, I don't want to — please, I want to wash your curtains and beat the carpets. I want to shine our shoes and the floors and I want to cook — I love to cook, because it's exciting for me. It tastes good to me and I can see your leathery skin turning pink and I take great pride in my work. I'll do anything, but I don't want to work."

"But I'm working, too, Miss Doris."

"But you had a higher education, Mr. Ernst, and so did your parents. And you have books on your bedside table and an education and an understanding of the things that you're dealing with, and you like what you do, and it doesn't cost you anything or very little, and it gives you enjoyment. But Therese and I have to pay for our enjoyments and we have to pay for them with money. I too know those Lippi Wiesels who write their own books and do all this talking about themselves and have this admiration for themselves, even though they have no money. But tell me please, what should I admire in myself? I don't want to work."

"But you enjoy working around the house."

"I do everything around here. It interests me, because it doesn't cost anything. That's different. Should I work as a cook or a servant — for the Onyx kids — Madam, dinner is served, Madam — no way, you could get fired, you have to brownnose her and that's why you have to hate her — you have to hate anyone who can dismiss you, even if they're good to you, because you work for them and not with them."

"But Miss Doris, you're working for me too, when you cook for me and when you wash my curtains."

"I'm working for you because I enjoy it, not because I'm afraid I won't be able to make a living. I'm not really working. I just do it like that" — leave me alone with your stupid lectures, I don't want to work and I want to keep my fur coat.

He brought me a silk scarf with an incredible pattern — "I thought you might like it, I think it would go well with your brown dress." But he's so good to me.

But he's so decent.

"My dear little Doris, my dear little Doris, my dear little Doris — I bet that's how they come up with a new song that becomes a hit."

"Is your grenade splinter still wandering, Herr — "

"Please call me Ernst."

"Er — I can't. Perhaps if I had my mouth on that grenade splinter, I can't possibly image that I could."

"You're a decent person, Miss Doris."

That's what he said. And I can believe what a man tells me for a change, okay?

"You know, Mr. — Ernst — that linoleum in the parlor — I was waxing it today, it's practical no doubt, because the dust, but it's cold somehow — "

"Do you think we should put a carpet?"

"You don't think that would be too much of an expense? If not, I would not be in favor of it."

"Let's look at carpets."

So we went to look at carpets together and I was allowed to meet him at the office and he took my arm in front of his colleagues, real official. It wasn't dark yet, either. I love him — not like that — but like that.

Well, maybe like that after all. With emphasis on love. Sometimes I get this funny feeling. My poor fur. Please stay out of my personal affairs, Mr. Green Moss. Fur, you stay. I wonder if he doesn't find me attractive. As far as I am concerned I don't want to want, but I want him to want it. I'm feeling so stupid, like I want to look at myself in the mirror all the time. So she had long legs. But so do I. And what they had in common — but our walks with dogs at trees and stars and grenade splinters that wander, do they mean nothing at all? And the leftovers from that goose lasted forever. Having a goose in common, isn't that worth something? And it lasted such a long time and didn't smell at all. Always he's talking about his wife. Will he never stop? What do you mean blonde — it's just a color. And Schubert and Baudelaire and — *Das ist die Liebe der Matrosen.*

His skin is getting more yellow every day, it's as if spiders were running over it, it's gross — we're talking real yellow with gray in it. I can't believe a compote made from fresh mirabelles wouldn't help. Why do all the jokes I know have to be so obscene that even a decisively decent woman, especially one in such highly decent bright yellow circumstances, couldn't possibly tell them?

He kissed my hand. He, mine. And without hesitation. I had left flowers on the dining room table. And then he left some for me.

Sometimes every night spent by yourself is a waste. But otherwise I'm fine.

I'll do anything, anything at all, but I won't work.

A letter. My God, a letter came. The mail comes at ten o'clock. I already know about the green ones that have advertising in them for shaving utensils and Rhine wine and free theater tickets that are a lie, since you have to pay for the show after all. Plus we have enough of our own theater around here. But there's a white one and it's closed in a mean way and that makes me suspicious. Who's that bitch writing by hand?

"Doris, I'm so grateful that you're here!" That's what he said to me yesterday. It's my apartment, my curtains, my cooking, my leathery skin of his. You, you belong to me — not because of money and a sofa to sleep on — I'm not lying, I'm not lying: please lose your job. I'm going to keep cooking — me and you — I'll continue to take care of you — I of you — I'll do laundry for people, I'll take the Onyx kids for a walk in parks and along rivers with fallen leaves, I'll type, I won't work — but I will do it for us — don't worry about losing your job, just go ahead. There's a white letter with edges that makes me suspicious — of course I open it, I'm the lady of the house.

And it says:

"My dear Ernsty: I hurt you and I was bad to you. You won't be able to love me any longer. But perhaps there will come a time when you won't be angry with me anymore. I so much want to explain to you: see, my entire life, before I knew you, was a constant battle, a constant back and forth between success and failure, a tense wait for the next day, a constant change between a good mood and depression. Things were happening all the time — and when nothing was happening, then you could be sure that something particularly beautiful would happen tomorrow or the following week.

"And then my work at the dance academy — I was so happy every time that I had made some progress. How sad, how desperate was I when I thought I had come to a standstill. How beautiful it was to cross the street, catching words and gestures of passersby or a ray of sun on a pot of geraniums — those myriads of things that happen in the street, they turned into a tune in my head that I could feel in my entire body. (Did you know that I always wanted to dance under that big curved blue neon sign at the subway station?)

"And then there were more disappointments and the fear of not reaching one's goal and I was tired on those days where I had just enough money to pay for thin tea and a dry roll. No, Ernsty, life wasn't always beautiful, but it was colorful and lively and full of change. And then came that tacky spring, so sweet and so soft, that season that makes you melancholy and lonely when there's nobody around whom you can love. And there you were all of a sudden, and nothing mattered to me anymore except our love. I was so happy and felt so safe surrounded by your kindness. And when we got married, I was so happy and proud that I had plans and a profession that I could sacrifice to you.

"And then I couldn't keep it up. The first year things were lovely and nice, the second year I desperately wanted things to be lovely and nice and I lied to myself a little. During the third year, I was really struggling and gritting my teeth. And during the fourth year — Ernsty, I almost went crazy. I was dying to go back to my thin tea and my dry roll and all that hope and expectation and that ability to create something out of my inner self. And I was terrified that those quiet uneventful days would be all that was left for me, until the end of my life. And I was scared to grow old, scared to have missed out on something. And because you were so good to me and did everything for me, you just didn't notice that I wasn't happy. I also felt so stupid being one of those endless variations of the 'misunderstood woman.'

"I just had been standing on my own feet for too long already, had lived with a profession I loved for too long.

Perhaps you could have helped me, we could have talked about it — that's the most stupid thing you can do when you're married, to keep your mouth shut to avoid hurting the other person. That always goes wrong. Too much accumulates.

"And then I met — well, we were talking about dance and all of a sudden, it came over me: it's not too late yet — but it could be too late tomorrow. And I was in love with him too. Yes, I was. And only now I know, it was already too late — now I know that over the years you have become stronger than everything else. I'm thinking about you a lot. I wish you well from the bottom of my heart. You won't want to write to me, but I wanted you to hear from me — well, you've already heard enough from

Your Hanne."

That's women for you. Stuck the letter under the cork carpeting. Of course she put her return address, it's under the cork carpeting too. I'm so agitated.

I'll do anything for you, my dear person, anything. Please lose your job.

We went to the movies together. It was a movie about girls in uniforms. They were high-class girls, but they had the same problem I have. You love somebody and that brings tears to your eyes and gives you a red nose. You love somebody — it's nothing you can understand. It doesn't matter whether it's a man or a woman or God.

It was very dark — he won't take my hand? I put it close to him — why won't he take it — I breathe his hair — where is that wandering grenade splinter? Am I the movies or love? *Das ist die Liebe der Matrosen* . . . I would sell the fur coat, if I could get paid for it in the currency of being able to touch his hair just once.

The movie is pulling me away from him, it's so beautiful. I'm crying. There are lots of girls — would you despise me — you're crying yourselves. You love a life or a teacher in the style of a cloister or you love a Green Moss or your future — am I any different from you, dear girls? He's not taking my hand.

"Doris, do you see that girl to the left — she looks like my wife, if only I knew where she was — can you see her?" Yes, she's under the cork flooring.

Good night, Green Moss — I'm too tired to go to sleep. I just got up from writing and walked over that spot on the cork carpeting, where she lies. That way I'm going to trample her to death.

My dear Green Moss, I drank from your cognac — do you think I'm ugly — don't I have anything to offer to you? Blue eyes. Tired. Because it takes a tremendous amount of strength not to open the door that is white and right next to me. Good night. No good night at all. You're all right, snoring away in your grief, while I'm lying awake with my happiness.

If you're human, you have feelings. If you're human, you know what it means if you want someone and they don't want you. It's like an electrified waiting period. Nothing more, nothing less. But it's enough.

It's a wonderful life. It could be even more wonderful, but already it's so wonderful that I don't have much to write in my book any more. He didn't talk about his wife at all all night. We were dancing in his apartment. But in a very elegant way and without any pressure. And the only reason I'm writing about this is because he didn't pressure me. And I'm bathing with lavender and press my clothes. A bit of color on my lips and I look in the mirror. Well, how do I look? I've tried myself out a bit by sitting in a café and I had an enormous effect, because you always get the most offers when you don't need them. But it does make life difficult if you really like someone and you don't feel like meeting anyone else and it turns you off and doesn't change anything. And he's not even my type.

I'm slightly drunk — I want him to be happy and I want him to notice and not notice that I want him to notice it. *Vienna, Vienna, only you, Vienna* — we were sitting there listening to the radio. Oh, it's so beautiful. *Das gibt's nur einmal, das kommt nicht wieder — das ist zu schön um — Wien, Wien, nur du allein — Wien, Wien, bist du ein Rhein — denn man macht Musik mit dir —*

at moments like these, I feel like a poet, I can rhyme too, within limits of course, and I become a rhyme — *Wien, Wien, nur du allein* — God, I'm so drunk — *Wien, Wien nur du allein* — he poured me a cognac to get to my senses but in order to get rid of it in an elegant way, I would have to go to the bathroom, which means walking through his bedroom — I can't walk in a straight line anymore and I'm awake with my new morality — it's no fun going for a carousel ride in your own bed. But to put it bluntly, I resent having to walk through the bedroom of the man I love, just to throw up. So I prefer to write instead.

Found a bottle of seltzer and finished it — feeling better already.

I want to be a joy for him and distract him from his thoughts about his wife who's lying under the cork carpeting and singing Schubert. And cooking alone doesn't do the trick. But my thoughts want to sacrifice something for him. So I'll get my life in order and my papers. And then he says: "It won't work, Doris, you can't just take something. There has to be an order to things and that order exists only if one person protects the other." I'll think about it. It's about the fur coat. I stole it. But now I love it — just as Ernst loves his wife. My fur coat has such soft hair and it has been through so much with me, sometimes things that were very difficult, but then there are small things we have in common as well. If Ernst forgets about his wife, I promise to forget about my fur coat. But it's not really the same thing because his wife left him, and my fur coat would do no such thing. If I abandon my fur coat, I'll wrong it.

The Green Moss is good to me. And he read my book, which shows me as someone who does lots of crazy things and whom you can't trust and there's so much I want — who can tell me what to do?

I would love to go dancing again. We would have to go together — and as I go to the bathroom, a guy accosts me — I tell him: Who do you think you are! I'm not free! And I'm one of those checkered cabs — are you free? — of course not, can't you see that the sign is flipped over? I would love to live with my sign flipped over for a very long time. And I don't mind if we're not doing well because we would be together — don't worry, we're not alone, we can always laugh about something — we'll always find something to eat, just watch. I could become a star, if only I became one for him. It's so hard, all of that. Perhaps he would give me an education.

I'm going to do it — my mother knows the address — I'm writing the letter:

"Dear Madam:

Once I stole your fur coat. Naturally, you will be mad at me. Did you love it a lot? I'll have you know, I love it a lot. There were times where it lifted me up and made me a high-society woman and a stage and the beginning of a star. And then there were times when I loved it just because it's soft and feels like a human being all over my skin. And it's gentle and kind. But I also had problems because of it, you better believe it. And I almost went as far as turning tricks, which is something a decent girl who wants to maintain her reputation shouldn't do. I want to return the fur coat to you. It's in perfect condition. I've always taken it off beforehand. My friend Tilli also treated it with great care. I want to believe now that you should not steal because of order and what have you. If I knew your face and I liked it, I wouldn't have done this to you or at least I would have felt sorry for it. I don't know your face, but I imagine you being overweight. That's why I don't have a bad conscience. It's only because of order and my papers and because of the sacrifice I have to make, and because I want to be taken and out of love. Perhaps you have other fur coats, even an ermine one. It's always the wrong ones who get everything. Please be good to my fur coat — please make sure it doesn't suffer when you sulfur it. And I can tell you that a thousand fur coats could rain down on me, because anything is still possible for me, but I would never love another coat the same way I loved this one.

Sincerely yours,

Doris

P.S. I'm sending this letter and the coat to my mother. She will give them to you. I'm sure she knows your address, because of course you made an incredible fuss that night at the theater. There's nothing in it for you if you report me to the police. But I'm going to have terrible trouble and it would destroy me. So there's no point in doing it."

And so I took care of business.

Love for love's sake is exhausting.

I haven't mentioned the letter to the fur lady yet. Just hinted at it.

"It's really hard on me, Herr Ernst. Can you understand that it is particularly those things you stole with your own hands that you love the most?"

Says he: "But you don't want to be a thief, Doris, do you?" Thief yes or no, it's a nasty word, but can't he understand me? We're so different. We could kiss some time, but what else could happen? I'm no thief. But I'm going to believe him.

"Silly girl," he says. I know, I know. Is he feeling sorry for me? That sort of thing just kills a man's sensuality. I sure don't want to get into all sorts of smooching in my book, but I feel very funny and there's something of an earthquake happening in my head.

And I'm making my rounds going shopping for him. It's so nice. There are small toy trains with children and a warm chilliness that makes my heart sing and train tracks and lots of stores and the sun is shining. And on *Bergstrasse*, there are lots of stands and booths — Herr Schlappweisser, the smoked herrings — mandarin oranges, oranges and cooking apples — toothpaste on the street — a blue post office with mailboxes — twenty-five pfennigs for four bananas, twenty-five pfennigs, bananas from the Canary Islands — a booth that sells sausages — the air is so brown, it's white and blue like lace for kitchen cabinets — take some, young lady, go on, take some — that's a colleague, she's from the office — What? Welfare. Welfare. Everybody is welfare — a colleague, she's looking pale like a dirty towel — buy pins, a pack of sewing needles. *Im Prater blühn wieder die Bäume* . . . he's wearing a yellow arm band with three black dots on it and playing the harmonica — Jim is playing the harmonica — I think that's the song they were playing when I lost my virginity — it's been a long time — *Im Prater blühn wieder die Bäume* — my God, that song's so old — Herr Ernst, if only you could come with me sometime. There's the underpass with that yellow mosaic, sometimes you can hear the train thundering over your head when you pass through. I always hurry because I feel like it's about to fall on my head.

Wenn wir beide — take some, young woman — those beautiful fuzzy felt insoles — take some, ladies and gentlemen — that's the kind of putty, super porcelain putty. Recommendations from here, recommendations from there — *Friedenau, Wilmersdorf, Steglitz,* all the western suburbs are driving me crazy with their letters of recommendation — beauuutiful mimosas, the hardy flower, beauutiful yellow ones, the plant for winter, that one can take anything, that one can take three pairs of ironclad male boots — take some, young lady — young lady — that kind of street has something in it, it makes you feel pregnant with something. If only we could walk down that street together sometime. But they only have it in the morning, that kind of street only happens in the morning — and there's so much life and people. And people who walk around in the morning in the fresh air tend to be unemployed and don't have anything.

"That street life you see these days — it's all about unemployment," says Herr Schlappweisser — "that smoked herring has caviar in it — anything else? Lemons they have next door — Franz, watch out, the lady here has her eyes on your golden fruits of the south."

And I'm having so much fun — there's this stand that sells salmon and then there's old Kreuzweisser, that's Karl's father, the one from the waiting room who I always got along with so well. I talk to him about his son. And he's just as nice and as cheeky as his Karl. And he's got a jolly tummy and wears a white coat like an abortionist. And I always buy something there for Ernst. Some kind of pink salmon — he can't be making any money on that. "Say hello to your son for me, Herr Kreuzstange." "There's a billet doux for you from that childish boy, young lady, do me a favor, don't seduce him, he needs all his strength for his job, as does everybody these days."

And Karl writes to me: "You still got your ambition — kiss my . . ."

Always those unelegant invitations which I heartily respond to. And I showed the letter to Herr Ernst and we both laughed about it, even though I was embarrassed because of the obscenities in it.

It's okay to cry by yourself, but the most wonderful thing is if two can laugh about the same things.

But we don't really enjoy the same things.

There's this shiny desire in me to sing — *Das gibt's nur einmal, das kommt* . . . and I know no Tchaikovsky, only songs and no Schubert — but my skin is singing. He kissed me on my neck, which just so happens to be my most sensitive spot. And so many wonderful words — you just can't think about them, they run through you like sparkling water. I'm completely gone and otherwise I feel like I'm ill with a fever and a stomachache — *Doris, dear little Doris, my little* — that goes right through me.

And again nothing. I can't let on that I want to, because that's just going to deter him — but oh God, I want to sing, I want to dance — *in die Welt hinein* — *Mein ist die schönste der Fraun* — *mein jam.* . . .

So he asks me if I had never been afraid of getting sick or pregnant, that was so dangerous for me. My God, you can't worry about everything! If you start that way, you're going to drive yourself crazy. You just have to hope that you'll be lucky — after all, what else are you going to do? You could just as well be thinking about death all the time — that seems impossible too — just like the other thing — it would be the same, actually. I won't believe that I could be dead until I'm actually dead — but then it'll be too late and nothing to be done about it — but until then, I'm just going to live.

And then he kissed me on that spot on my neck — that's life. By the way, now I think he's gorgeous. He has this gentle smile on his face like a pediatrician. He has tiny black dots in his eyes. Sometimes I want to insult him, so I can love him even more — because then he would show his honor through his anger or his elegance through his gentleness — one or the other — it would be equally wonderful to me. Of course I don't really want that to happen.

Father thou art in heaven, please make my inside so good and so fine that he can love me. I'm going to buy him a tie, because that's something I can do. Someone once told me that I have an almost masculine understanding of it. I guess there are situations where having a past is to your advantage. Heavenly Father, perform a miracle and give me an education — I can do the rest myself with make-up.

I've thought up a surprise for him and purchased several candlesticks painted in ochre. Very subdued with a reddish floral-style pattern — and candles, also in muted colors and lots of them. Because he loves candles. I think that's stupid because you have to use so many of them to replace electric light. I love it when a room is well lit, except when I look as ugly as I did four weeks ago. But not anymore. My cheeks have a first-class natural pink shimmer to them. Tomorrow I'll prepare the surprise for him, together with vases full of cyclamen. I've saved up too, you know. With a great deal of effort I have refrained from smoking those ten cigarettes for six and have sold them to Herr Kreuzweisser at five, who then resells them together with his salmon at six. Apiece. And then I'm going to illuminate.

I had also planned to embroider something, but it didn't come out. I slightly damaged the cushion on the cork carpeting. He didn't notice — which is the best part of it. If only he has patience — I'm getting an education — if he only has enough patience, for heaven's sake.

I'm at a fast-food restaurant at *Joachimsthaler Strasse.* It's called "Quick." That's American. And everything is so fabulous and happy. In an hour, I'm going to pick him up at his office. I asked him: "Will this be bothersome to you?"

"Of course not."

"Are you sure?"

And then he says: "I've always wanted to ask you to

pick me up, but I thought it might be too much of an effort for you to go into town just for that." And he doesn't notice how much I want to. Could it be that that not noticing is love after all? When you're in love like this, you're no longer sure about yourself. And because you're so afraid to do something wrong, you're sure to be doing just about everything wrong. Or at least you're completely different from the way you want to be, because you're so full of love and anxiety — and you want to be a good person and the real you without any tricks or premeditation. And none of the usual bullshit, and you don't want to think, just be nice and kind. And nothing else. Can a man take that? I'm going to dare show my love though.

And I prepared everything. I put my letter to the fur lady and the tie that goes with his bluish-gray suit on the table. I did a tremendous job mending his shirts, but I won't put them there. I love him so much now that I don't care if he notices how much I struggled to fix his shirts. And perhaps that's true love. And then the cyclamen — they're a little cold but nice. And all of those new painted candlesticks with candles in them. I'm going to meet him at the door and say: "Just a moment please." Then I'll go and light them — and I say: "Please. I prepared a cold supper for you and have filled tomatoes with my own hands. They're a bit smeared with mayonnaise on the outside, but still much cheaper than at the store. And brisoletts and an arrangement of rolls with something on them and a piece of useless parsley and a leaf of lettuce on the side. That's for elegance." How do I deserve to be this happy?

And now I'm at Quick — I love those automatons so much. I pulled for myself shrimp and Westphalian ham — there are lots of dishes where the name tastes the best, because when you're German that always gives you this air of traveled superiority, and I used to know men who grew taller, as if someone had shoved an invisible pillow under their butt, just because they would order Italian salad, just because of the Italian. I couldn't even finish the sandwiches I had pulled — but what a fairy tale this Berlin is — that automaton. And then I sit here by myself and all I can feel is: I'm going to go home soon. I have to look at all the people that fill up the restaurant and — are you going home? Please, I don't have much time. I'm going to meet someone any minute to go home. I'm a decent woman, and every word I utter is about my love for the man in my life.

I had a cup of coffee and had the bathroom attendant curl my hair. Just in case. And I gave her an additional 20-pfennig tip — I'm going to tell him that. He gave me 5 marks — I want to return four of them to him. Otherwise I'd feel like I'm taking advantage of him. I never used to think about where men get their money from. I always had the impression that they just have it, from transactions and things like that. And then you don't care. But when you know how someone makes his money and you watch him get up early in the morning and all that, that gives you some consideration. Dear God, thank you — I have to go.

Berlin is all covered with snow. It makes you drunk. You wake up and everything is sugar-coated. It's snow and you get it delivered for free. It's so beautiful, it makes me tremble. Sometimes I would think that he found me disgusting. We had all those candles — and my letter about the fur. So he says: "Doris, are you doing this for my sake?"

So I got angry. "Yes, of course — did you think it's because of that fat old lady?" And then there was all that sentiment in the air and such terribly oppressive excitement, so you know in your bones: something's happening. Things are starting to get all blurry.

"No," he says. "No, no, no — I like you far too much, little woman." Like or no like — Herr Ern — I just couldn't say his name — all the cyclamen were looking at me and the air was piercing — "You, Herr — I'm not innocent, you won't be responsible for me, I have gratitude and lo — well, you know — and you don't have to marry me and you can forget me again — and if — well, okay, you would be as much pleasure for me as I would like to be for you."

Those words were coming out of my mouth like an energetic prayer, but my arms and my heart were all weak and helpless. My voice was trembling and I had to cry, but I wanted to, because that sort of thing always gives a man reason to come closer. And then we comforted each other until we were terribly happy, and this morning we saw the snow together for the first time and woke up together.

That's not what love is all about, I'll have you know, but it's part of it, in a nice way.

Spring. It makes me terribly uncomfortable, but he wants to buy me a coat on the 15th. I'll take the cheapest they have. Until then, I'm going to keep the fur. Otherwise I couldn't go outside. It's still quite cold out. He told me about countries where they already have flowers this time of year.

I don't talk much. I'm very careful. For a woman it's different. Once she's all crazy about a guy, she doesn't really care anymore. But with a man, you can destroy everything with one word that's out of place. I'm very much afraid because of my lack of education. That really estranges you from each other, once things start to become erotic. Because you've known each other for so long before that. That gives you a feeling of embarrassment.

He brought me lots of flowers. Life is so beautiful that it's starting to become a religion for me for the first time in my life. I don't mean to say that I'm pious — but it's holy to me, because I'm so happy.

Mother! I've fallen apart. Dear mother. It'll pass. I can't cry anymore. It happened tonight — my hand is lame, dear notebook — I'm just going to spill everything now. I've been unhappy many times, but it always passes. Does it really? What an ordeal. Perhaps I should take my own life. But I don't think so. I'm much too tired to commit suicide and don't really want to do anything with myself.

I'm sitting at the *Friedrichstrasse* Station. This is where I arrived a long time ago together with the politicians and this is where I end — damn it, no, I won't even think about it. I still have enough food in my stomach for another three days.

Sometimes all sex is good for is so you can learn to say "du" to each other — and that's always been difficult for me to do. But it was a sign. At seven o'clock tonight, he kissed me — very carefully on my arm — with a kind of love that was no longer sensual. I felt like praying — thank you God, thank you — is that really me? — so happy — "Dearest" — and that fear inside of me — is that how you kiss me? — there must be a mistake, and it was — "Hanne" — he says — "Hanne" — I got all tense and didn't let on anything. I had love inside of me and anger that turned my face to stone. Then he starts to cry — it's an outburst like that Trapper's. I touch his hair and say: Dear, dear. Some of them only need a few minutes to make you feel a hundred years old. He loves her that much. There's nothing you can do about it. I can understand, if he forgets me — I would have done the same thing for him. My pain was so immense, it didn't hurt anymore and I had lost all my bright yellow. And it was my fault. After all, a decent man is a child, and the masculine responsibility falls on the woman. He's good. I destroyed everything. With love. Life really is a bitch. But he was so unhappy. If I couldn't be his love, I had to get him another one. I'm dizzy.

So I say: "Just a minute." I secretly take my suitcase and put it in front of the door. I forgot some of my things, which I couldn't really afford to do. But I really can't allow myself any feelings at all right now. And it's nighttime. And on an envelope I wrote his address, which also used to be my address. And I put the letter from under the cork carpeting inside. And I sealed it with blood from my heart. "Do you have a stamp, Ernst?" I ask. "I just want to mail a letter — no, please let me go alone."

We'll never go for walks again, I'll never be frying kidneys for him again — and I really didn't want to make much of a to-do about it, but I did want to kiss his hand just once: you gave me the most wonderful time of my life. Yes, I can get really nasty, but sometimes I can also be very decent. Even though it's the stupidest thing you can do. I could have cut myself into pieces, if that had made you love me, I — oh my God. I'll never see you again. I want to kill myself in front of your door tomorrow. Bullshit. Now I'm writing it all to you as in a letter — I'll mail it to you, or maybe not — it doesn't matter. But talking to you this way makes me feel better. What torture. But you experienced that too, because of your wife. But I don't even know what I should live on. That's a big difference. I'm still only the girl from the waiting room. I kissed your hand and your hand had such careful fingers that didn't dare touch a woman, because they thought she would break if they did. And so I left. And I almost had to throw up on the stairs, that's how miserable I felt.

Here I am again. It's all over. Over forever. I borrowed some money from the concierge, because I need some for what I'm planning to do. You'll give it back to her, I told her. I didn't want to take advantage of you, I swear. There's still some of it left. For half of it, I bought myself something alcoholic. I'll return the other half to you tomorrow. Unless I'm very hungry, then I don't care what a man thinks of me. Now that whole rigamarole is starting all over again.

And then I went to the address under the cork carpeting. It was a very elegant restaurant in the *Westend*. She was dancing there with her man. I sit there like a rock. And I don't care about anything — the way the waiters stare at me and all that. I can see that Hanne. She looks like she had dance lessons and a good family and her mother gave her castor oil when she was little, and a piece of chocolate afterward as a reward. That's the kind she is. When I was 10 years old, I had a friend for three days. Her name was Hertha with a th. She wasn't allowed to talk to me, because I only went to the lower-level school and I knew where babies came from. But she was older than I and would always ask me.

And that Hanne was dancing in a sweet way and waltz-ing and a blue Danube — and she was blonde. I was sit-ting there and I know my man and my apartment, which is hers. It was very strange. And she was wearing an ivory georgette dress with lots of little pleats and red straps and a red belt. Not very stylish, but so innocent. And she's not even all that beautiful, just blonde. Her legs aren't all that long either. And she smiles at her man like a stone in a graveyard that's been hit by a ray of sun. The man is very elegant and has black oily hair, the kind that can never make you happy because it always shines for someone else. I'm drinking one cognac after the other, very quickly. There's so much that's broken in me. I can't keep going like that. I'll talk to her during intermission. It's a tiny room where we sit, very narrow.

"Your husband sends me. You should come back to him — please go now, now."

At first, I wanted to add: or else he'll die — but then she would have become arrogant again right away and assertive and Ernst wouldn't have had the upper hand anymore. She had dry wrinkles around her mouth and scared eyes like Tilli had sometimes and like she's going to break into tears any minute. God, you really can't take them seriously those girls, they're such babies — espe-cially if they're blonde.

I have enough money — I'll have another cognac.

I almost have to laugh now — she couldn't get a word out. She must not have been doing too well! And that jealous way she looked at me — that pleased me, I guess it means I'm pretty again. I wasn't jealous of her at all, because you're just not with an old hag like that.

So I just asked her: "You'll go right away, won't you?"

And she says "Yes." And talks to me as if she were dreaming, or else she wouldn't have been that honest: "I can't go on living like this — and a man with a stable income who loves you, and whom you don't love too much, that's still the easiest way to live, and it's a nice thing too, if you can give someone pleasure."

I didn't love him too much. And I wasn't able to give him pleasure. But I'm not going to let on to that cork-carpet woman that I'm hurt. And then she says: "It's so tough out here."

It sure is. As I leave and close the door behind me, I'm once again filled with sadness. Of course it's difficult. So she wanted to become a star at her age, and still hasn't managed to do it. And now everything is back in place and my candles are burning — I'm going to get — I — I still have enough money — I'm having another cognac — oh God.

I had a conversation. A guy with a cardboard box comes up to my table. I wanted to be alone with my grief.

But he's on his way to Ohligs, which is near Cologne, that's where his uncle lives who has a smithy and he needs help.

"Why are you crying?" he starts up.

"I'm not."

"Of course you are." And so one word leads to the next.

I say: "I've just witnessed the sad fate of a friend of mine." And I tell him my story. He smelled from manure. That instilled confidence in me.

He had a sister once who had the same sort of thing happen to her. And I was lucky that I got out in time. It only would have gotten more boring and I would have gotten older and didn't have the right interests and I always would have lacked education, and he would have gotten sick of that some day. Especially those gentle ones, they want intellect — and there I would have been with my lack of knowledge — and would have wasted my best years. And he could relate to that kind of error, with a man who was something better, as a girl. Because times really are bad. But true feelings — you should have those only with your own kind, otherwise things don't work out. But that's exactly my problem, that I don't have any of my own kind. I don't belong anywhere. And they would just use you. But he certainly didn't do that. He was a decent man. That didn't matter, in any case, I was stuck in the mud and it was my own fault.

And he had four ham sandwiches in his cardboard box — his mother isn't doing so well, but she made those for him because of the trip and because it's nighttime. He gave me two of them. I didn't want to take them — but he said I shouldn't insult him, because we were a chip off the same block and you had to start sharing at some point, and with him, I could allow myself to have feelings without any calculation. He didn't mean feelings in an indecent sense. Out of curiosity, I asked him if he would marry my kind. So he said that there was a lot about my past that bothered him, and those educated types were more tolerant in that respect, but it would be a possibility. And we had a conversation. I asked him what I should do now, whether I should start turning tricks. He wasn't in favor. And I told him about the office and the fur. He said it would be stupid of me to return it — better sell it and have my mother send me my papers, or perhaps have new papers made. He gave me an address of someone who does that for people. He's been through a lot too, but now he wants to have his peace and quiet. Perhaps start his own business with a friend — he thought my case was a tough one. But ultimately, the honest way was the best way to go.

And there was so much I still wanted to ask him — but he had to catch his train. And he was biting his lip and said it really stunk that you couldn't really help anyone these days if you didn't have money, and he was all pale with fury. And we shook hands. I spit at him three times, I had learned that from our director at the theater — he says: "Stop it. That's bullshit. What's that supposed to mean?"

I would have loved to have given him something to take on his journey, but all I had left were thirty pfennig and my spit. I did pull ten pfennig worth of roasted almonds for him from the vending machine. He says: "You're crazy. Get on to your waiting room or else they're going to steal your luggage that consists of nothing but bullshit."

That's just the kind of thing Karl would say. Karl always wanted me. When I come back to my notebook, I find a one-mark piece stuck between the pages. Can't believe I didn't notice how he put it there! He had so little. I'm sending him a thank you, all red with shame. I would like to be good to somebody.

At home my candles are burning, I had painted the candlesticks so decoratively. For several pages now, I've been trying not to think of it, but I have to think of it — if he were only to have one sad thought about me once in all his happiness, that would make me so glad. I would love to call him sometime — but what for? It's possible I would disturb them in a situation, but a decent person wouldn't do that. I wish I could think of him as a nasty person, that would make it easier — but he was decent. And it was beautiful. Pain is pain that destroys everything that could have been happy. But it can't destroy what has been beautiful — can it?

I want to get to the Zoo station waiting room — maybe Kreuzstanger's Karl will be there. I would very much like to ask him to give me some time without sex. You have to be able to wait, especially with a woman. I wonder if he'd understand. I'll never get used to one without education which is where I would belong — and one with education is not going to get used to me. But I can't just walk down the *Tauentzien* and with the big industrialists, I just can't be with a man right now. It's just like it was with Hubert — because my body is a lot more faithful than I am. Nothing you can do about it. But it'll pass, I'm sure. For now, my sensuality is in prison. That's love. Someday, it's going to be released.

It's not that important, really — I'm a little drunk — maybe I won't go to the Zoo station waiting room. Instead I'll go to an elegant dark bar, where you can't see that my eyes are dead with tears — and I'll let myself be invited by someone and nothing else — and I'll dance, dance, dance — I so much feel like dancing — *Das ist die Liebe der Matrosen* — we're only good or bad when we love, or we're nothing at all for lack of love — and we don't deserve to be loved, of course, but otherwise we'd have no home at all.

I'm going to go look for Karl after all, he always wanted me — and I'll say to him: Karl, let's work together. I will milk your goat and stitch eyes on your little dolls, and I will get used to you with everything that's involved — but you have to give me time and you have to leave me alone — you have to let these things take their course — and if

191

you don't want to, if you don't want to, then I'll have to do it on my own — where should I go? But I don't want anyone to kiss me. And I've had enough of the office — I don't want to go back to what I had before, because it was no good. I don't want to work, but I have buoys of cork in my stomach. They won't let me go down, will they?

Dear Ernst. In my thoughts I'm giving you a blue sky, I love you. I want — want — I don't know — I want to be with Karl. I want to do everything together with him. If he doesn't want to — I won't work, I'd rather go on the *Tauentzien* and become a star.

But I could just as well turn into a Hulla — and if I became a star, I might actually be a worse person than a Hulla, who was good. Perhaps glamour isn't all that important after all.

ABOUT THE AUTHOR

Irmgard Keun was born in Berlin in 1905. After a stint as a stenographer in Cologne, she started training at the local drama school. Her acting career culminated in an engagement at the renowned Thalia Theater in Hamburg.

In 1931, at age 21, she published her first novel, *Gilgi — a Girl Just Like Us*, the story of a stenographer who sacrifices her professional ambitions for a passionate love affair. Her second novel, *The Artificial Silk Girl*, appeared only one year later, and instantly became a bestseller.

With the rise of the Nazis in 1933, Keun's books were blacklisted. The author left Germany for Belgium in 1936, and later for the Netherlands, where she met fellow exiles Stefan Zweig, Ernst Toller, Hermann Kesten, and Joseph Roth. Keun published three more novels in exile. In 1940, the Nazis conquered Holland, forcing her to return to Germany, where she survived the war in hiding.

After the war, Keun continued her literary career but enjoyed only modest success, until her early novels were rediscovered and reissued in the late 1970s—in the wake of the feminist movement in Germany.

Keun refused the many invitations to document her tumultuous life in an autobiography. She died in 1982 in Cologne.